RETRIBUTION

Roy Burnett

First Published in 2025 by Roy Burnett

© Roy Burnett 2025

The right of Roy Burnett to be identified as author of this work has been asserted in accordance with the Copyright, Designs and Patents Act 1988 and the Copyright and Related Rights Regulations 2003

This is a work of fiction. Any references to real people, living or dead, real events, business organisations and locations are intended only to give the fiction a sense of reality and authenticity. All names, characters, places and incidents are either a product of the author's imagination or are used fictitiously, and their resemblance, if any, to real-life counterparts is entirely coincidental

Cover design by Craig Lee

Book layout & typesetting by Lumphanan Press
www.lumphananpress.co.uk

Printed & Bound by Imprint Digital, UK

ISBN: 978-1-8384079-1-9

'In its purest form, an act of retribution provides symmetry. The rendering payment of crimes against the innocent. But a danger on retaliation lies on the furthering cycle of violence. Still, it's a risk that must be met; and the greater offense is to allow the guilty go unpunished.'

— *Emily Thorne*

List of Main Characters

Ahmed Salah bin Saud – Saudi Arabian Prince
Andrew Fox – Ex-army captain working for the MOD
Anna Larsen – Norwegian Prime Minister
Aziza Halimi – Secretary at Beaumont Oilfield Services in Algiers
Billy Flanagan – Scottish oil industry worker
Brig John Stevenson – Head of Special Forces in UK
Col. John Jamieson – Pentagon liaison officer
David Wallace – Prime minister of UK
Farah Halimi – Daughter of Aziza Halimi
Giles Rankin – Operations director at the Ministry of Defence
Graham Fraser – Head of SO15 Counter Terrorist Branch
Jamal Nasir – Saudi security services chief in London
Jasmine McAdam (Jaz) – Wife of Rory McAdam
Jeff Smith – Military attaché at the British embassy in Beirut
Jody Miller – Apartment owner in Aberdeen
Johan Olsen – Norwegian businessman and head of the Sovereign Fund
Julia Monet – False identity used by Farah Halimi
Kari Olsen – Daughter of Johan Olsen and university student
Khaled bin Ahmed Al Hussein – Saudi security services chief in Paris
Lars Newburg – Norwegian ambassador in Lebanon
Layla Barrack – Mossad agent in Beirut
Martin Ingram – MI6 Middle East chief
Ramiz Rafik – Palestinian doctor
Robert Taylor – Aberdeen estate agent
Rory McAdam (Mac) – MI6 Field Operator
Saladin – Code name for CIA asset highly placed in Mabahith
Steve Foley – Head of MI6
Sven Solberg – University student and boyfriend of Kari Olsen

Glossary of Terms

ADDSS – Algerian Secret Service
Extérieur – French word meaning outside
GIGN – French Counterterrorist Police
GPS – Global positioning system
Hezbollah – Lebanese armed militant group
IED – Improvised explosive device
IDF – Israeli Defence Force
Isha – Muslim evening prayers
ISIL – Islamic State in Levant
J-SOC – American Joint Special Operations Command
Kaffir – Arabic for a non-believer
Mabahith – Saudi Arabian secret service
MOD – Ministry of Defence
NATO – North Atlantic Treaty Organization
Salaam alaikum – Arabic greeting: Peace upon you
Shukraan sadikee – Arabic: Thank you, friend
SO15 – British Counterterrorism Police
Tais-toi – French phrase meaning shut up
Wadi – Dried-up riverbed

PART I

Chapter One

Rory McAdam sat on the bench holding his silenced handgun against the ribs of the notorious Saudi Arabian prince, Ahmed Salah bin Saud, wealthy arms dealer and middleman channelling millions of dollars into ISIS hands. The Saudi prince had followed explicit instructions to attend the meeting alone and knew better than to defy the notorious assasin he had hired. In the darkness of night and the heavy downpour of rain, the prince could not see that the man sat next to him was MI6 agent Rory McAdam and not the assasin Ali Hussein Al-Sabbah.

After several circuits of the square and seeing nobody, Mac was sure that he and the terrified Saudi were alone on this pitch-black October night. Alone in the darkness and torrential rain. Rain that had been accompanied by a crashing thunderstorm that kept the people of Beirut inside their homes, warm and dry against the worst storm this region of Lebanon had seen for several years.

Unknown to the MI6 operator, he was being watched and filmed by Layla Barrack, Mossad's top undercover spy in Beirut, using the latest camera technology developed by the CIA to covertly enhance the scene with infrared light. Layla Barrack had been the agent responsible for identifying Ahmed Salah. The head of Mossad had passed on the information to MI6, which now allowed Mac to finally draw a line under the dirty business of money and arms supply to several notorious terrorist organisations. ISIS had seen its funding dry up abruptly and had then been destroyed by a combination of British, American, and Russian aerial bombing, and persistent ground attacks from Kurdish and Syrian troops on the ground. The Kurds and Syrians made strange bedfellows and would resume fighting each other again at some point in the future but were proof of the old adage, 'My enemy's enemy is my friend.' The Kurdish fight to rid themselves of ISIS was the supreme objective. The battle against the hated Syrian leader Bashar Al-Assad would wait until another day.

Layla Barrack lay hidden across the front seat of her car, covered by a blanket, breathing hard and trying to stay motionless in the darkness as Mac made three circuits of Martyrs' Square in downtown Beirut. Layla sensed his approach each time even though his advance was silent. He carried out three circuits using all his army and MI6 training to ensure he was alone before his meeting with the Saudi, Ahmed Salah bin Saud. A meeting which left the Saudi dead on the bench, wet with his own urine from the loss of control in his bladder. Twenty seconds after his neck was punctured, he was dead, paralysed by a lethal injection of poison.

The meeting and slaying of the Saudi prince had been secretly filmed by Layla using the hi-tech night-vision scope attached to a mobile phone, which gave enough detail to provide a clear picture of the killer. Layla did not question this highly risky intrusion but followed her orders from her Mossad boss in Tel Aviv as she always did. For most of the ten minutes they sat on the bench, Layla could only see the back of the British agent, but when he removed his arm from the victim's shoulder and rose from the bench, picked up the two holdalls, and turned around, Mac had looked directly into her lens, giving her a clear, full-on picture of his face. Mossad had a valuable piece of film of a British government-sanctioned execution.

* * *

Nobody in Lebanon could have foreseen the devastation that would be caused that fateful afternoon when a fire broke out in Warehouse 12 at Beirut port. The Hezbollah militant group had been using this warehouse to store a vast quantity of weapons and ammunition for their ongoing terror campaign against Israel. It was well known that ammonia nitrate was an explosive mixture extensively used in the mining industry and as an agricultural fertiliser. It was also the chemical of choice for a wide range of terrorist organisations employing IEDs, improvised explosive devices.

The two Hezbollah operatives were aware of the volatile nature of the goods being stored there and took precautions to limit the risks. Smoking was absolutely forbidden and only permitted in the so-called 'safe area'. In this part of the warehouse, there were pallets stacked with hessian sacks which had been ignored ever since any Hezbollah operator had set foot in the warehouse. Unfortunately, one of the Hezbollah men on duty on that fateful day had finished his coffee and flicked his cigarette butt away, totally unaware that it landed in the middle of a pile of the hessian sacks and smouldered away, setting the dry hessian material alight. The resulting small fire then ignited a huge collection of fireworks which quickly spread throughout the warehouse complex.

The fierce blaze spread unchecked, causing 2,750 tonnes of ammonia nitrate to detonate, resulting in catastrophic damage to the port area and much of downtown Beirut.

Apartment blocks, hospitals, shops, and office blocks were destroyed in a matter of seconds. Cars were thrown into the air and smashed to the ground. Streets were filled with smoke, dust, and broken glass as people screamed for help. Over 200 people were killed and more than 7,000 injured, along with a staggering $70 billion worth of damage. So ferocious was the blast that not a single pane of glass remained in a two-mile radius from the warehouse storing the explosives.

The blast shook the whole country of Lebanon. It was felt as far away as Turkey, Syria, Palestine, and Israel, as well as parts of Europe. It was heard in Cyprus, more than 240 kilometres away, and was one of the most powerful non-nuclear explosions in history.

The moment of the explosion was when Layla Barrack's luck ran out. Sitting in her beautiful downtown apartment in the central district of Beirut, with views over the sparkling azure Mediterranean, she began downloading the video of the assassination of the Saudi Arabian prince Ahmed Salah bin Saud from the previous evening. She had been trained by Mossad to use the dark web to transfer any material through a series of secret sites in various European countries before it was automatically rerouted back to the Mossad headquarters in Tel Aviv.

Her modern apartment in the Seaview tower block was situated on a small hill overlooking the beautiful Zaitunay Bay, constructed to give maximum views of the Mediterranean sea and the Beirut corniche leading to the iconic Rouche sea rock. The huge glass windows in her sixteenth-floor apartment gave

Layla fantastic panoramas but offered no protection from the massive blast from the dock area less than a mile away.

The windows on the north and east faces of the tower block shattered instantly as the shock wave of the blast hit the building. Layla was flung against her back wall by the explosion, killed instantly and bleeding from almost every part of her body. The glass came in with such a force that it shredded her face, leaving her blind and deaf to the catastrophic event that ended her own and many other lives in the carnage of downtown Beirut that day. The city looked as if it had been carpet-bombed and the howl of ambulances and fire engines filled the streets of Beirut for many days.

Chapter Two

'Come and join the Beaumont family and you'll learn new skills, be well paid, and have the opportunity to travel the world.' This was the opening line of the sermon from the big Texan with the booming voice. His recruitment drive around Angus included a visit to Fintry High School in Dundee where he addressed the teenage boys and girls soon to leave school. The message burned into Billy Flanagan's mind. He clung to every word and knew from that day onwards, without doubt, he wanted to become an oilman. To join the thousands of other Scots presented with the golden opportunity of a career in the oil and gas business.

Beaumont Oil Services was one of the oldest and most famous oil and gas service companies in the world. It was owned by the O'Malley family, who could trace their oilfield roots back to working on the Spindletop oil gusher of 1901, which had started the oil boom in Texas and fuelled the American industrial revolution. Beaumont Oilfield Services, or BOS as they liked to be called, had developed oil-well cement, and Sean O'Malley, the son of an Irish immigrant, had been smart enough to patent various tools and products associated with oil-well cementing.

BOS grew into a national oil service company with bases in Louisiana, Oklahoma, California, and Alaska, as well as its original headquarters in Texas. Further expansion saw the O'Malley family develop internationally, first in Canada and then Mexico and South America. To capitalise in the North Sea oil boom of the late seventies and early eighties, they took the decision to open a manufacturing plant in the small rural town of Arbroath, in the region of Angus, fifty miles south of the fast-developing European oil capital of Aberdeen.

Although many so-called experts questioned the company's decision to locate this far south of the oil capital, there were sound strategic decisions behind this thinking. First, it gave Beaumont a large factory with a five-year rent-free holiday, courtesy of Angus Council, and second, it gave them access to a pool of cheap, skilled labour in the Angus region, desperate to join the gold rush taking place up north with the huge salaries that were synonymous with the oil industry at the time.

* * *

Three months later Billy had left school and joined Beaumont Oil Services, travelling thirty miles each day by bus and thriving in his new environment as he learned the engineering and technical skills used to mix and pump cement into an oil well.

With his thirst to learn and progress, Billy immediately impressed his employers and embraced the opportunity to enter the oil industry. Beaumont did not employ the traditional British system of apprenticeships but used the American method of quick learning and rapid advancement for those who listened and learned. The American boss in Arbroath took a shine to Billy though struggled at times to understand his thick Scottish accent. He liked Billy's work ethic and his quiet temperament. Whenever there was a need to work over a weekend or a public holiday, Billy was inevitably the first to stick his hand up and volunteer. From his early years, Billy Flanagan was earmarked to go far at Beaumont.

Billy Flanagan harboured a dark secret that drove his passion to make an impression with his employer and find a way out of Fintry and the negative feeling around Dundee at the time. The city had been infamous for being run by left wing socialists who turned their back on the North Sea oil industry and even rejected a plan from Ford to build an engine manufacturing plant which would have provided employment for hundreds of men and women in the area. Billy's father had been a union official and a driving force behind the industrial suicide in the region.

The other blight on the Flanagan family was Billy's older brother Michael Flanagan. Billy had been forced to accompany his mother to Edinburgh High Court to listen to the prosecution give graphic details of his brother attacking an old-age pensioner and robbing her of her £26 weekly pension. The woman had been pushed to the ground by Michael Flanagan and punched in the head until she was forced to release her handbag containing her precious pension. Excessive alcohol and drugs consumption were the only excuses given by Michael Flanagan's defence lawyer.

Billy dreaded the day of his brother's sentence as he sat in the public gallery with his mother and listened to the judge after a unanimous guilty verdict from the jury. 'Michael Flanagan, do you have anything to say before I pronounce sentence?' Billy's brother stood motionless with his head bowed and gave a slight shake of his head. 'Nothing, not even sorry to the poor defenceless and frail woman who spent four weeks in hospital because you were desperate to steal her weekly pension?'

The judge waited in vain for a response before slowly shaking his head and sentencing Michael Flanagan to twelve years in prison. His mother sobbed quietly in shame as the courtroom began to empty.

Since the day his brother had been convicted for attempted murder, Billy Flanagan had suffered bullying and persecution back in Fintry. He rarely left the house other than attending school and became a social recluse. Billy dreamed of leaving Dundee and starting a new life far away from the shadow of his notorious brother.

* * *

When called into the manager's office one day, Billy trudged up the steps, trying hard to think what he had done wrong. His timekeeping was good now that he had his own car, and his engineering skills had blossomed under his supervisor. He was confused and nervous as he knocked and entered the manager's office.

'Sit down, Billy. Would you like a coffee?'

Billy shook his head and mumbled 'No, thanks,' still trying to think what he had done wrong and dreading what was coming next.

His manager continued. 'We're pleased with your progress. You're a fast learner, and we're very impressed with your work ethic. How would you like to join our international squad and work overseas?'

Billy looked his manager in the eye and took a few seconds to analyse the question he had asked. For a young man born in Fintry, and desperate to leave Dundee, this was the equivalent of winning the lottery. He could barely contain his excitement as he replied, 'Yes, I would love to serve Beaumont overseas and will go anywhere you need me. I'm ready whenever you say.'

The manager smiled back at him, happy with his response. 'We have an urgent need for technicians in Nigeria, Billy. Do you think you're up for it? You'll work as a trainee field engineer.'

Billy started shaking his head in turmoil. 'Nigeria?' He leaned over the desk, trying to control his excitement, and responded. 'Thank you for the opportunity. I won't let you down.'

Two weeks later, an elated Billy Flanagan from Fintry, Dundee, climbed the steps at Dyce airport, still in a state of astonishment, with a brand-new glossy passport in his hand, and boarded a plane for the first time in his life, embarking on a career as a trainee engineer on the oil rigs. He was determined to make the most of this golden opportunity.

As his plane descended into Lagos airport, Billy looked out the window in wonderment. The six-and-a-half-hour flight from London had transformed the scene to a contrasting cocktail of recently built offices, modern highways, and apartment blocks in the city centre, fringed by ramshackle houses and endless jungle as far as the eye could see. *Wow*, Billy thought. *You wanted to see the world, and here we are.*

* * *

A five-year stint in the oilfield centre of Port Harcourt saw Billy slowly evolve from a trainee engineer into a skilled and dedicated team leader. Life in Port Harcourt, with money in his pocket, also saw him develop a lifestyle involving copious amounts of booze and prostitutes during his time off. The oil rigs in Nigeria were mainly situated on land or in shallow river deltas which meant no long-distance trips and very few overnight stays for Billy Flanagan so more time to spend at the bar and with the hookers. Over time his manager and fellow workers saw him grow aggressive and contemptuous of the local Nigerians employed by Beaumont and a string of complaints eventually triggered a meeting with his country manager.

'Billy, you're a great worker, your attitude on the rig is great, and the customers really like you. However, there's a growing list of complaints about your behaviour towards the locals and we've taken the decision to transfer you. This is for your own good, and the good of your fellow workers. I've arranged a posting to Algeria for you.'

His manager waited for this to sink in before he added, 'My buddy, Don Fletcher, is the country manager there and is really happy to get a guy with your skills and knowledge. I know you'll do a great job.'

He leaned forward and spoke in a fatherly tone. 'Before you head up to Algeria, Billy, I need to give you some advice. You may see me as an old fart, but I have nearly twenty years of experience working overseas, and you need to remember this: wherever you are, you're a guest in *their* country. Treat the locals with respect and decency.'

The manager stood up and held out his hand, although he was having serious doubts over whether his advice would be heeded. Billy was courteous in his reply. 'Thanks. I've enjoyed my time here and it's probably a good time to move on.'

Chapter Three

Algeria was a place that Billy had barely heard of. He had seen an old film of Beau Geste and the Foreign Legion, but reality only set in after he arrived in Algeria. His first meeting with Beaumont country manager Don Fletcher didn't go well. Fletcher was a religious man, a practising Christian, who abhorred swearing and could not hide his distaste when someone took the Lord's name in vain – as Billy Flanagan did on a regular basis. However, Fletcher recognised Flanagan's experience and technical knowledge and gave him the role of resident engineer, responsible for all repair and maintenance of Beaumont's cementing equipment in Algeria.

'Welcome to Algeria, Billy. The culture and customs here are very different from Nigeria and you will have to quickly learn and adapt to how we do business. This is a Muslim country and although alcohol is available, we recommend discretion.' Billy nodded his understanding, although he was confused. *It's either a dry country or it's not. What's to be discreet about?*

His new boss continued with one more piece of advice. 'Because you are working in a Muslim country, you may come across local women working in some offices. This is a relatively new change in Islamic culture, and you must never approach or engage woman in conversation unless they talk to you first. Is that clear?'

Billy nodded and replied, 'No problem, Mr Fletcher. I'm a fast learner and the desert will make a nice change from the jungle or offshore Africa. Hopefully there are no snakes or mosquitos here.'

Don Fletcher gave him an apprehensive smile and raised himself half off his chair, holding out his hand. 'Good to have you aboard, Billy. Keep your nose clean and listen to the experienced guys already here. The staff house is close by, so find an empty room and get settled in. You'll be travelling to our service base in Hassi Messaoud tomorrow morning with our cement supervisor Alec Spencer.'

The next two years saw Billy carry out an excellent job under very difficult circumstances where the extreme heat, lack of spare parts, and language barriers stretched his abilities to the limit. The conditions in Nigeria had been difficult too but had been alleviated by the endless supply of cold beer and local bar girls swarming around the foreign workers. No such comforts were available in the oilfield town of Hassi Messaoud where Billy was based. He was very popular at the rig sites, where he kept the equipment running through a mixture of improvisation and practical engineering. Over time, Don Fletcher eventually recognised the value of Billy Flanagan and turned a deaf ear to his constant use of industrial language with a strong Scottish accent. His written reports were basic in the extreme, but his value for maintaining the Beaumont equipment was priceless and made a big contribution to the overall profitability of Beaumont in Algeria.

* * *

When Billy received a call to take a local flight up to the head office in Algiers and see Don Fletcher, he feared another dressing-down for his language or his poor paperwork and was pleasantly surprised to be met with a smile and a warm handshake. 'Billy, I think it's fair to say you and I have not always seen eye to eye, but I have always recognised your contribution to our success here in Algeria.'

Fletcher paused to let the compliment sink in. 'I'm pleased to say you've been offered a promotion to the engineering supervisor's position in Libya. It's a big step up for you.' He paused again. 'Your paperwork will have to improve, and you need to ease up on your swearing. But I'm sure you can do it.' He gave Billy a backslap and a hearty,

'Congratulations.'

Don Fletcher laid on a farewell party in the Beaumont staff canteen, which he asked his wife Susan to help make the arrangements for. Thursday afternoon was the beginning of the weekend in Algeria and around thirty of Beaumont's staff attended the party to celebrate Billy's promotion and transfer to Libya. Among those attending the party was Don Fletcher's attractive Algerian secretary, Aziza Halimi, a shy, soft-spoken Algerian woman of twenty, smooth-skinned and slim, with beautiful big eyes, and long, dark, silky black hair. During his occasional visits to head office, Billy ignored his boss's warnings and had tried asking her out on a date several times, but Aziza, much to Billy's disappointment, had politely declined each time. Aziza was also the niece of the vice president of the state oil company Sonatrach, which ensured she was looked after very well by the management of Beaumont Oil Services.

Being a strict Muslim, she stuck to apple juice as the party turned from a late-afternoon food and wine social gathering to a drinks party with music and dancing. Aziza Halimi politely declined the many invitations to dance, instead preferring quiet chit-chat with her office colleagues. Billy had changed from beer to vodka and his annoyance at being continually turned down by Aziza festered inside him.

He waited until she was alone before joining her at a table and engaging Aziza in casual conversation. Waiting until she had excused herself to attend the washroom, he looked around and, satisfied that nobody was looking in his direction, he reached inside his pocket, withdrew a tiny bottle of clear liquid, and quickly tipped the contents of the bottle into the apple juice she had left at the table.

The Rohypnol had been supplied by one of the many drug dealers that frequented Billy's council estate in Dundee during Billy's last trip home. After returning from the toilet and taking a few sips of her apple juice, the effects of the Rohypnol were almost immediate as a heavy fatigue overtook her. She turned to where Flanagan was sitting, watching her experience the results of the drug. She stood up. The room started to spin, and she swayed unsteadily on her feet as she spoke to him, slurring her words. 'Billy, I'm sorry, but I don't feel well. I must go home.'

Billy gave her a sympathetic smile. 'No problem, Aziza. I'll escort you home to make sure you're okay.' They walked slowly towards the door, unnoticed by most, except for Don Fletcher's wife, Susan, who glanced over as Flanagan slipped his arm around Aziza's waist to support her as she wobbled out of the door.

He helped the heavily drugged woman into his room, locked the door, and laid her onto his bed. Flanagan was so used to paying women for whatever he wanted that he became disillusioned into thinking women found him attractive and desirable. He could not and would not accept that Aziza continually rejected him. As he started removing her clothes, he thought, *Now is the time to show her what she's been missing.*

Early the next morning, Billy Flanagan, hungover with a raging thirst and a feeling of guilt, slipped out of his staff house, climbed into the waiting taxi, and headed to the airport for a morning flight to Tripoli. He looked out of the back window with a touch of remorse as the taxi pulled away, swearing he would never set foot in Algeria again.

Several hours later, Aziza awoke in a strange bed in an unfamiliar room. Dazed with a pounding headache and in a growing panic, her mind screamed out in confusion as to how she had got here. She had no memory of the previous night and panic grew to sheer terror as she pulled back the sheet to find herself naked with spots of blood on the bed sheets where she lay. She slowly moved her hand down to her groin and screamed as she held up her hand, sticky with blood. She became hysterical as her mind began racing, trying to think back to the night before and how she'd ended up in this strange bedroom. She picked her clothes up from the floor, dressed quickly, and let herself out of the empty apartment. Outside, she looked back and recognised the building as the Beaumont staff house but could not remember how she'd got there.

As she opened the door of her home, she was greeted by her stern-faced aunt, who immediately asked, 'Where did you stay last night? You normally tell me if you're staying over with friends. We were worried about you.'

Aziza was so ashamed that she lied. 'I stayed over with one of the girls from the office. I'm sorry I forgot to tell you.'

Her aunt considered her reply and decided to let it drop. 'Okay, go and get changed. We're going to the mosque for Friday prayers.' With that, her aunt turned and walked away, still not convinced but wanting to avoid a family argument.

A few weeks later, Aziza was being sick most mornings and was having trouble getting to the office on time. Her aunt noticed her longer spells in the bathroom and could not help hearing the retching on the other side of the door. The aunt's concern was growing day by day before she finally made up her mind to confront Aziza. 'Come and sit down, Aziza. We need to talk.'

Aziza had known this moment would come sooner or later and it was with a mixture of relief and dread that she sat down opposite her aunt.

Before she could ask a question, Aziza burst out crying, tears rolling down her cheeks as she sobbed. 'My periods have stopped, I'm always sick, and I'm so tired.'

Her aunt had looked after her since both her parents had died in a car crash when Aziza was a toddler. 'What is happening to me?'

Her aunt shivered as thoughts went through her head. 'Let's go and see the doctor. She'll prescribe some medicine for you. Come on. I will drive you there.'

Aziza was still weeping as they drove to the doctor who had looked after the family since she'd graduated from medical school.

Aziza nervously held on to her aunt's arm as she shuffled into the doctor's room. 'Bonjour. Salam alaikum,' the doctor greeted them in the curious mixture of French and Arabic used by most upper-class Algerians. 'What can I do for you today?' Aziza sat in silence, staring at the floor. She had told no one about the rape. She had no sexual experience and felt humiliated and ashamed.

Her aunt spoke first. 'Her periods have stopped, and she feels unwell, constantly tired, and she's being sick a lot.'

The doctor frowned and turned to look directly at Aziza. 'Aziza, when did you last have a period?'

Aziza's head was beginning to spin in confusion now. She paused for a long time before replying in a barely audible whisper: 'Three or four months ago, I think.'

The doctor immediately sensed the woman in front of her was panic-stricken and tried to calm her nerves. 'Aziza, I need to examine you and do some tests.' She opened a drawer and withdrew a clear plastic bottle. 'Can you go into the bathroom and fill this? I need to check your urine.' She handed the sample bottle to Aziza, who returned a few minutes later with the bottle half full.

The doctor unscrewed the cap and inserted a paper into the liquid. After a few minutes, she removed the paper and held it up to a coloured chart. The doctor looked at the result and let out a discernible sigh before speaking directly to Aziza. 'I will have to do some more checks, but I can tell you now, without any doubt, you are three months' pregnant.'

Her aunt groaned and looked first at Aziza, then the doctor. 'You are absolutely sure, yes?'

The doctor was a long-time friend of the aunt and knew how devastating this news would be, not only for Aziza but the whole family.

She nodded as she replied. 'Pamira, I would not speculate on such a serious matter. Aziza is pregnant.'

Chapter Four

The father of the baby remained a mystery to Aziza, her aunt, and her uncle as they tried to trace her movements for the previous three months. Up until now, Aziza had led a quiet life and only socialised with a few close friends at weekends. Her aunt was convinced it could only have been the evening she had attended the office party for the farewell of the Beaumont employee and had stayed out all night. Aziza continued to insist that she had no knowledge of being with a boy but did confess to her aunt about waking up in a strange bed, naked among bloodied sheets, in a room that she found out later had been occupied by Billy Flanagan prior to his transfer to Libya.

Don Fletcher attended regular meetings at the Sonatrach office in Algiers and after a routine oil-well planning meeting was quietly asked by the Sonatrach vice president, Mahmoud Babouche, to accompany him to his office on the executive floor.

'I need to meet with your field engineer – a Billy Flanagan. I understand he has transferred to Libya, but I need you to arrange for him to fly back to Algiers for a meeting on a private matter.'

A perplexed Don Fletcher did not want to antagonise the vice president of Sonatrach, his biggest customer in Algeria, but needed to know why he should be making this strange request to management in Libya.

'It's a private family matter that involves this man.' The VP paused and leaned forward with his palms held out towards Fletcher. 'If you value your company's business here in Algeria, you will make it happen.'

Don Fletcher knew there was trouble ahead. He had discussed it with his wife over dinner that evening. 'I'm in a very difficult position. If the Libya office refuses to send him, or he refuses to come, I may have to take this to my boss in Houston. But I don't know what the issue is. He refused to elaborate other than saying it was a *private family matter*. What's that supposed to mean?'

Susan Fletcher put down her fork and knife, supressing the uncomfortable feeling in her stomach, and drew a deep breath. 'You remember the office party you put on for Billy Flanagan? You mentioned the secretary Aziza has often been late getting to the office since then, claiming that she's sick.'

Fletcher looked at his wife in silence, bracing himself for what was coming next. 'The girl, Aziza – the VP's niece – left the party early with Flanagan and she didn't look right. She was a bit unsteady on her feet for a girl that had been drinking apple juice all night.'

She paused to take a sip of water. 'I thought it was strange at the time but didn't feel the need to mention it to you. I'm sure her sickness relates to that night. Call it a woman's instinct, but I think she must have been forced into sex against her will.'

Don Fletcher's mouth was agape in shock, 'You mean—?'

His wife finished the sentence for him. 'Yes, rape. I can see it a mile away now. If only I'd intervened when they were leaving the party.'

* * *

Predictably, Billy Flanagan refused point-blank to return to Algiers for any meetings and immediately started looking for a job outside of Beaumont. After Flanagan's rejection to return and face the music, Susan Fletcher had arranged a discreet coffee with Aziza Halimi's aunt.

'Let's be honest with each other, woman to woman, mother to mother. If Aziza's in trouble, I will do anything to help her. No girl should be left to face this without support.'

The aunt knew she could not keep Aziza's condition a secret forever and it came as a relief that Susan Fletcher understood the situation with her niece. 'For the family's sake, and for Aziza, we want her to go and stay in Paris and have the baby there. It would be best for everybody.' Pamira Babouche wiped away tears from her cheeks, feeling a weight had been lifted from her shoulders.

Don Fletcher knew he had no alternative but to take the issue to Beaumont's management in Houston. He flew to a high-level meeting in the boardroom chaired by CEO Jim O'Malley, grandson of the founder of Beaumont Oil Services. The Algerian business for Beaumont contributed over $8 million per year to the bottom line and the forecast for the following year saw the revenue increased to $11 million. After hearing the full sordid tale from Don Fletcher and discussing the options, O'Malley summed up the way forward for Beaumont's business in Algeria.

'First, we fire that little bastard Billy Flanagan. Second, we provide first-class accommodation in Paris for the girl. Third, we will provide a monthly allowance of $20,000 to cover the expenses for the girl and the baby.' O'Malley looked around the table. 'Have I missed anything?'

Don Fletcher cleared his throat and caught the eye of

O'Malley. 'Sir, what about schooling for the child? If she stays in Paris, the costs will be expensive for a single mother.'

O'Malley thought for a few seconds before continuing. 'Good point, Don. Tell them we will cover all education costs, wherever she raises the kid, up to leaving university, if that is acceptable.'

Don Fletcher flew back to Algiers the next day and went straight from the airport to the office of the Sonatrach vice president. An anxious Fletcher laid the document down on the desk in front of his customer, longing for some sign of acceptance.

'I have secured an excellent financial support package for your niece. I hope this will meet with your approval and enable us to draw a line under this most distressing event.'

The vice president did not reply but gave a slight shake of the head and a grimace before picking up the document and reading slowly through each item. Finally, he lifted his head and looked into the eyes of Don Fletcher.

'Thank you, Mr Fletcher. This is a very generous compromise under the circumstances. This will of course remain confidential between you and me. Please pass on my appreciation to Mr O'Malley and I hope to see him again at next year's oil show in Houston.'

With that show of acceptance, a relieved Don Fletcher stood up, shook hands with his very valuable customer, and left the room more relaxed than when he had entered.

Chapter Five

Five months after arriving in Paris and settling into her comfortable apartment in the exclusive Les Halles area, Aziza Halimi, accompanied by her aunt, entered the private wing of Paris's exclusive Saint Leopold maternity hospital and after a difficult labour, Aziza gave birth to a healthy baby girl. While she recovered in the hospital, her aunt registered the baby under the name 'Farah Halimi' with the birth certificate showing William Flanagan as the father and his occupation as petroleum engineer.

The French registrar lifted her head from the registration page and paused. 'Farah Halimi? Not Farah Flanagan?' was the question she posed to the aunt. 'This is most unusual here in France. The baby will not take the father's name?'

The aunt stared back with a determined look and furrowed her eyebrows. 'No, she will not have the father's name. Please enter the name Farah Halimi.' Her tenacious and determined demeanour left the registrar in no doubt and without further debate, she entered the name into the computer.

Before returning to Algiers, Aziza's aunt went to visit an agency recommended by the Algerian embassy in Paris. After reviewing applications and checking references, she hired a French nanny to move in with Aziza and help her raise the baby. Young Aziza had no experience of raising a child and was completely unaware of the difficult times and sleepless nights ahead. The nanny turned out to be a masterstroke and was a great help in guiding the young and inexperienced single mother, alone with a new-born infant in Paris. Raising a young child in another country was a very difficult task for young Aziza, so the experience of the French nanny was crucial. The nanny herself had three grown-up children and showed great patience and fortitude in helping Aziza develop into an excellent mother.

* * *

The day before Aziza gave birth, Billy Flanagan received a phone call from the human resources department of Qatari-owned oil service company Al Wasad confirming his application for the position of lead engineer in the cement department had been accepted. Flanagan gave out a shout of joy mixed with relief that his three-month quest for a job had finally been successful. He had been mystified at the negative responses he had received from the numerous attempts to find employment since being abruptly terminated by Beaumont.

Unknown to Billy Flanagan, Beaumont had contacted all other major American and Canadian oil service companies, advising them to steer clear of any employment applications from UK national William Flanagan. No specific reasons had been given by Beaumont, but many companies shared a 'blacklist' network for troublesome employees.

By the end of that week, Billy had a one-way air ticket on Qatar Airways to Doha, a three-year work permit, and a salary almost double what he had earned at Beaumont. The cementing department of Al Wasad had been started from scratch with a very generous budget from the Qatari owner Sheikh Khalifa bin Hamdan, and Billy Flanagan was amazed at the vast amount of equipment for him to maintain and service. Most of his work in the early days was for contracts offshore in the giant Dome and North Dome gas fields. The Qatari government had a policy of offering huge subsidies and openly encouraging local companies to grow, expand, and generate profits, both within the country and internationally, and Khalifa bin Hamdan had made full use of this governmental financial support.

After founding their cementing business in Qatar, Al Wasad spent the next few years establishing a good reputation and, over time, began to develop further into the Middle East: first, into Bahrain, followed by bases in Oman, Abu Dhabi, Saudi Arabia, and Egypt. Billy Flanagan was very good at his job and within a year was promoted to regional engineer, travelling to all the bases of Al Wasad, repairing and servicing their equipment. His work did not go unnoticed by the management, and he was summoned to a meeting by the regional director.

'Billy, you're doing a great job, and we want to show our appreciation.' Billy began wondering what was coming next. 'Our business in Egypt is continuing to grow and we have new opportunities in the pipeline. We want you to go to Cairo and manage our current business and help to expand our services in Egypt and North Africa.' Billy's mind was in turmoil at the mention of North Africa. He had visions of being asked to go to Algeria and the mere thought of it sent shivers through his body.

'Well, what do you say? It's a great opportunity for you and there are many British and American expats in the oil business there. I'm sure you'll meet new friends and enjoy a new challenge.'

Billy quickly thought through the options and found that, in reality, he had very little room to manoeuvre. Refusal would be the beginning of the end with this company, and he remembered how difficult it was to find a job after being terminated by Beaumont. Billy broke into a smile as he gave him his answer. 'That's great news and I accept the offer. I will do my very best for the company and won't let you down.'

Home for Billy turned out to be a large apartment in the exclusive district of Maadi, a leafy suburb that ran from the corniche along the banks of the river Nile, to Wadi Degla, a dried-up riverbed ten miles inland. Maadi was home to many oil companies and their senior staff, as well as diplomats and upper-class Egyptians drawn by the cosmopolitan restaurants, cafés, bars, and shisha houses. The Association of Cairo Expats had established a social club complete with bar, which had become extremely popular as a watering hole with the many expatriate workers in the city. Locally known as the 'ACE Club', Billy Flanagan became a regular and a familiar face at the bar.

Billy threw himself into his new role and grew the business in Egypt, Tunisia, and Libya without ever needing to step foot in Algeria. Fortunately for Billy, there was sufficient turnover and profit generated from customers in these countries, along with additional work transported up from Sudan, that the dreaded subject of Algeria never arose during his meetings with his Qatari management.

Chapter Six

With the constant support of her mother, Farah Halimi had thrived at school in Paris and was an extremely talented pupil who excelled in all subjects. Fluent in French, English, and Arabic, Farah was outstanding in sciences and mathematics, and she was an excellent athlete, representing her school at long-distance running, swimming, and kick boxing. Her exceptional exam results had given her the pick of French universities. After careful consideration and discussions with her mother and great uncle, she chose a degree in Modern History at the prestigious Sorbonne.

Life in Paris for a young woman could not get much better with sumptuous Parisian restaurants and coffee shops and a wealth of historical sites and artwork to explore, but Farah had an unresolved issue that ran through her like an open sore. Whenever she raised the subject of her father, her mother would immediately clam up and tears of sorrow would lead to a rage inside her that remained for days. The shame and horror of that night ate away inside Aziza Halimi, and she became withdrawn as depression took hold of her life. No doctor's drugs could help her and at the age of thirty-nine, she died, a broken women who lost her youth and innocence at the hands of a monster. The autopsy found a high concentration of serotonin in her bloodstream but not enough to take her life. No other contributing factors were revealed during the autopsy and the death certificate stated the cause of death as *natural causes*.

For Farah, losing the only parent she had was heart-wrenching. She knew her mother had been a troubled woman who masked her feelings from her daughter and tried to bring her up the best she could as a single parent. A small funeral service was attended by Farah, two of her school friends, and her only surviving relative, her great uncle Mahmoud. As soon as he heard the news of the death, he had flown over in a private jet provided by the Algerian government.

Her uncle was now an old man, frail in body but still possessing a razor-sharp mind. Farah was anxious to find out more about her mother's early life – a subject that had been brushed over or changed at the first opportunity whenever Farah had asked her. She knew of her great uncle and her late aunt, but little else. Now that they had buried her mother's body in the Muslim graveyard at Bobigny, on the outskirts of Paris, Mahmoud Babouche sat her down in her apartment and started to tell her the story of her mother being raped and left pregnant as a teenager by a Scottish man who ran away, never to be seen or heard of again.

He told her of the guilt felt by the man's employer and the deal they had offered by way of compensation. Her uncle tried to explain it all in a sympathetic manner but could not hide his anger at the mention of the name Billy Flanagan.

Farah had been physically sick after hearing the story of how she was conceived and the circumstances of the world she had been raised in. Her poor defenceless mother, sexually violated and robbed of a normal loving life by a monster who resorted to drugs to force himself on her. Farah Halimi cried until there no more tears to give and as she cried, there grew inside her a steely resolve. A determination to seek retribution for her mother. Only vengeance could wash away the horror of her mother's past desecration.

Two months after the death of her mother, Farah received a letter from the Beaumont Corporation in America, full of sympathy but giving notice of the cessation of the monthly payments made to her mother's account. She was already financially comfortable and had just accepted a position in the administration department with the embassy of Saudi Arabia in Paris. Her fluency in Arabic, French, and English, as well as her first-class degree from the Sorbonne, had ensured an attractive salary package for the tall young woman. Her high cheekbones, flawless skin, and sparkling eyes gave her grace and elegance, and it was a confident Farah that started out at her first job.

Her boss at the Saudi embassy needed interpreters fluent in the three main languages in his business. Khaled bin Ahmed Al Hussein, the European head of Mabahith, the ruthless Saudi Arabian security service, had been tasked to gather intelligence on the many European-based opposition parties or critics of the Saudi regime. Al Hussein dedicated his life and considerable energy to ensure the continuation of the Saudi royal family's power base in the kingdom and abroad.

* * *

One Saturday evening, Farah and one of her ex-classmates from university were walking home from a café near the apartment they shared and as they turned the corner into a side street, they witnessed a teenage girl being attacked by two men. The girl was trying to scream for help, but one of the men stood behind her and held her tightly with one arm as his other hand covered her muffled cries. The second man was tearing at her clothes, trying to pull down her trousers.

The sight of this triggered deep and raw emotions inside Farah. Without warning, she launched herself at the man attacking the girl and snapped a ferocious kick to the side of the man's head, causing him to stagger backwards holding his eye and screaming in pain. Everything happened so fast, and the second man, shocked at seeing his friend reeling back holding his eye socket with blood pouring out through his fingers, released the teenager from his grasp. Farah moved forward, pushing the teenage victim aside, opened her hand, and swung a powerful punch with her palm, connecting with the man's chin and breaking several teeth which then bit halfway through his tongue. He could only emit a muffled gurgle from a mouth of blood and broken teeth as he collapsed to the ground.

The two girls who had witnessed the ruthless response from Farah differed in their reactions. The teenage victim was overcome with gratitude to the stranger who had come to her rescue and dealt with the two attackers so mercilessly. Farah's friend was horrified by what she had witnessed, shocked at the unexpected violence that came from a well-educated and quiet young woman she thought she knew well. Such was the distress it caused her, she left the apartment she had shared with Farah and moved back to live with her parents in a suburb of Paris.

* * *

Farah sat before her boss in a closed-door one-to-one meeting. Khaled Al Hussein leafed through her original application form, her appraisals, and her personnel details, with no hint of what was to come. The newspaper clipping on his desk reporting an attempted assault on a Parisian teenager had the headline *Heroine to the rescue*, accompanied by a grainy CCTV photo of Farah as she approached the side street. The article included an account of the events of the attack by the two unknown men and a description from the teenager of a young woman who'd come to her rescue.

He finally addressed her in English, holding up the newspaper clipping. 'Farah, our technicians back in Riyadh have run this photograph through facial-recognition software and confirmed the identity of the girl who fought off these attackers as you.' He paused, awaiting a denial, which was not forthcoming, so he continued.

'I am very impressed with your bravery and actions to help the girl. I need fearless and resolute staff members like you who can travel Europe, look like a European, and behave and sound like a European. Would you be willing to assist my operations here in Paris and in any other locations I might need you to go?'

Farah tilted her head slightly to one side and stared back at the man across the desk with a puzzled look. 'Excuse me, sir, but I thought I would be confined to the administration office here at the embassy. Why would I need to travel in this position?'

Al Hussein broke into a smile. 'Farah, as head of the embassy here in Paris, security of my country is one of the many responsibilities I have. All my staff here were born in Saudi Arabia. They look like Saudis, speak, think, and act like Saudis. You are a French-born Algerian, fluent in English and Arabic, and your family roots are in Islam.' He added, 'I also note your athletic ability and physical fitness too. Kick boxing is not an activity I would normally associate with a beautiful young woman like you. I can see you as a great asset to my team.'

Khaled took her relaxed smile and a nod of her head as a positive sign. 'I will be arranging additional training courses for you, which will involve overseas travel under different identities. You will be issued various passports under different names.' He paused and looked her in the eye. 'These are standard practices in our field of work. Are you okay with this so far?' Farah's head was in a spin at the thought of travelling on embassy business with false identity documents. He finished with the welcome news that her current salary would be quadrupled. In the back of her mind, she began thinking of how this opportunity would help her put an end to torment that had plagued her for so long.

Farah's acceptance of the new role triggered a flurry of courses in communications, current operations, and opposition individuals and groups considered to be a threat to Saudi Arabia. After a meeting between Al Hussein and his controller in Riyadh, they agreed to send her for specialised training with the notorious Algerian Direction des Services de Sécurité, normally referred to as 'DSS'. She travelled to Algiers using a Saudi Arabian diplomatic passport, driving licence, and credit cards in the name of Lina Ayad. The Algerian government having recently established strong links with the government of Saudi Arabia, including sharing of security intelligence as well as helping to manipulate OPEC oil and gas pricing and strategy, the DSS agreed to the highly unusual step of accepting a trainee from the security service of another country. Farah impressed her instructors during her classes on surveillance, countersurveillance, unarmed combat, electronic tracking, explosives, and firearms.

After completing her training with the DSS, Farah Halimi returned to Paris as a different person – a fully trained field operator with a glowing testament from her Algerian training team. Her hard work and dedication to take on new and difficult skills gave Farah a newfound confidence and belief in herself. She had regularly outperformed her male training colleagues in both classroom work and fieldwork and had worked seven days a week for the past ten months with little or no rest days. Upon her return to work at the Paris embassy, she wasted no time in applying for a well-deserved one-week holiday.

Chapter Seven

Saudi embassy regulations required Farah to fill in a holiday travel form, which included travel details, dates, and accommodation details when travelling outside Paris. She duly filled in all the details required for her week-long trip to Cairo and used the travel documents in the name of Lina Ayad as instructed by her boss.

A few weeks earlier she had logged into LinkedIn and entered the name 'William Flanagan'. After a long search with no success, she then typed in the name 'Billy Flanagan' and immediately received a response. Billy Flanagan was listed as the North Africa Area Manager for Al Wasad Oilfield Services based in Cairo.

Farah's blood ran cold looking at the name on the screen. She downloaded the accompanying photograph with a feeling of disgust bordering on hatred. She then searched the website of Al Wasad and found the contact details for the branch office in Cairo. Posing as an official from the contracts department of the Saudi national oil company Aramco, Farah had no trouble getting confirmation from the secretary in the Egypt office that Billy Flanagan would be in Cairo and available for a meeting during the first week of May.

The air ticket and hotel room at the Maadi Hilton were paid for through a discreet travel agency in eastern Paris, owned by the Saudi government. After arriving at Cairo airport and passing effortlessly through Egyptian passport control and customs, Farah caught a taxi to her hotel located on the banks of the river Nile.

Next day, she rented a standard non-descript saloon car at the car-hire desk at the hotel and set the satnav for the street where the Al Wasad office was located. For the next three days, she parked her car at different locations but always with a view of people entering or leaving the Al Wasad office. Her surveillance paid off as she began to piece together a lifestyle pattern for Billy Flanagan, who habitually left the office late afternoon and headed for the ACE Club in a taxi. His normal custom was two or three hours drinking at the ACE Club then a taxi home.

During Farah's fourth day in Cairo, she trailed her target again to the ACE Club where Billy had enjoyed drinks late into the evening as the next day was a Friday and the beginning of the Muslim weekend. Waiting patiently outside the club, Farah kept an unwavering eye on the front door of the club until Billy appeared alone just before midnight, swaying as he made his way to the rank of waiting taxis. Farah gave a silent prayer that he emerged alone as she made her move, getting out of her car and quickly closing the distance between Flanagan and the leading taxi.

'Hi, Billy. Do you want a lift home?' she asked.

Billy Flanagan stopped in his tracks and slowly processed what he had just heard, looking with hazy vision at Farah and smiling. 'Do I know you or is this my lucky day?' he slurred.

She turned on her charm. 'You don't know me, but I've heard of you, and I want to get to know you better,' she replied as she dazzled him with her smile and a slight giggle.

Farah took his arm and led him across the road to her hire

car, trying to keep him relaxed and reassured. 'Your place or mine for a nightcap?'

As drunk as he was, Billy immediately understood the question and its implications. There was no hesitation in his reply. 'Your place would be good. My place is a bit of a tip and there's no vodka left.'

She had been pretty sure that he would choose her place rather than his. 'No problem. My place it is then.' She unlocked the car, and he slid into the passenger seat, still trying to work out exactly how he was sitting in a car with a beautiful young woman, who was offering him drinks at her house, which would surely lead to even better things.

As the car pulled away, she turned to her passenger. 'My place is in Zaara Maadi, about ten or fifteen minutes from here.' Billy sat back and relaxed. He knew Zaara Maadi well and had visited customers there on many occasions, but never late at night, driven by a gorgeous woman.

He reached over as he put his hand on her thigh. 'Take your time. Tomorrow is Friday, and we are in no rush.'

Farah looked straight ahead, hiding her distaste at him touching her, and concentrated on the route she had rehearsed three times over the past few days. It was a lot harder in the dark, but she found the side road she was looking for. Billy looked out of the window and was puzzled to see a building site with a row of partially built houses.

Farah saw the perplexed look and reassured him. 'Don't worry, this is a shortcut. My house is just on the other side of this compound.' She drew up in the pitch-black of an unlit piece of waste ground. 'Come on. It's just a couple of minutes from here.'

He unbuckled his seatbelt and slid out of the passenger seat, almost stumbling with excitement and anticipation of what lay ahead. She took his arm and led him to the rear of the building site. Billy wanted to find out more about this mysterious woman who had thrust herself into his evening.

'How come you know me, but I don't know you?' he asked.

Farah ignored the question as she led him over to the spot she was looking for then stopped. She let go of his arm before speaking. 'You don't know me, but you once knew my mother.' Billy had a growing sense of confusion and mystery. Farah quickly continued. 'My mother was Aziza Halimi... from Algiers.'

The name and location sent Billy into a panic accompanied by an uncontrolled shivering all over his body and sweat running down his face.

Farah watched him in the light of the full moon as he took a step back from her. His bottom lip began to tremble as he held up both hands in some form of protest.

'I don't know anybody called Aziza and I have never been to Algiers.'

Farah reached into her pocket and felt the cold steel of her stiletto knife. She took a small step forward and closed the gap between them. 'Even now, you can't face the truth. You can't face the fact that you drugged and raped my mother and left her pregnant while you ran away and left her to a life of misery and sorrow. You disgust me, you coward!' His life flashed before him. It was too late to regret raping her.

In one swift movement Farah's blade clicked into place. Billy heard the click but didn't comprehend what the noise meant. She straightened her right arm and brought it up, slashing his throat with a bewildering speed as she sliced through the jugular vein, carotid artery, trachea, and oesophagus, causing a fountain of blood to erupt from his torn neck. Farah stepped back to avoid the red river pouring from his body. She missed the gurgling sound of Billy Flanagan's last words as he tried in vain to say sorry.

Farah was soaked in perspiration as she dragged the lifeless body of Billy Flanagan into the partially dug drainage ditch at the back of the building site. She covered the body as best she could, using her hands to push sand into the ditch. Half an hour of work saw the body covered enough to ensure anybody on site would miss it unless they started digging up the ditch. Besides, she had chosen her days carefully and the building site would be empty over the weekend before work resumed on the Sunday morning.

Farah returned to her hotel in the early hours. She showered and changed before checking out, handing back the keys to the car company, and catching a taxi to Cairo airport for a morning flight back to Paris.

It was a full two days after Farah's departure that Billy Flanagan was reported missing to the Egyptian police. His secretary had called his housekeeper to ask if she had seen any sign of him. His mobile phone had been called many times and gone unanswered until the battery ran out. Two days after the police search began, Billy Flanagan's body was found. Workmen arrived one morning and noticed a pack of wild dogs fighting among each other at the back of the construction site. As two of the more courageous workmen approached the dogs to find out what was causing the commotion, they reeled back in horror as they observed the remains of a human leg that had been uncovered. The scent of the decomposing body had attracted the hungry dogs from the nearby wadi where they now reluctantly and slowly returned to, constantly looking back at their lost meal.

PART II

Chapter Eight

Ramzi Rafik, a well-respected member of the medical community in the city of Nablus, headed up the medical centre located in the West Bank in Northern Palestine. Doctor Rafik had studied medicine at Cairo University and graduated with honours before returning to work in his home city and marrying his childhood sweetheart, Henna Yazad. Life in Palestine was extremely tough under Israeli occupation. A culture of resistance had turned many ordinary Palestinian people into extremists. Armed resistance groups sprang up, fuelled by hatred and violence.

Unknown to the doctor and his wife, their two teenage sons had been influenced by older boys and cajoled into joining the Palestinian resistance. They had become active members of the al-Aqsa Martyrs' Brigades and both boys had taken part in heavy street fighting against the Israeli Defence Force that had invaded the West Bank in an effort to curb the wave of suicide bombers entering Israel. The fierce battle for control of the area eventually ended with the Israeli army inflicting horrendous casualties on the Palestinian resistance fighters, including both Rafik boys, who had been slaughtered in a hail of rockets fired from an Israeli helicopter gunship.

The tragedy of losing both sons caused unbearable grief. After burying them in simple graves, side by side, facing Mecca,

Ramzi Rafik's wife Henna swore vengeance against the country that had butchered her beautiful boys. Murdered in the prime of their lives. She had gone to the mosque to pray and then began asking around as she sought out members of the Palestinian resistance movement. After a frustrating few days when everywhere she turned she was met with a shrug of the shoulders or a shake of the head, she was eventually told to stay inside her house and someone from the resistance movement would come to see her.

The next day, while her husband was working at the hospital, there was a knock at her back door. She opened it to find a stranger, accompanied by a man she recognised from her regular visits to the local mosque. She hesitated before opening the door and inviting them into her kitchen. The stranger spoke first. 'I hear you are looking to meet someone from Hamas. I can pass on a message to them for you. What do you want?'

Henna snarled at the stranger. 'I want revenge on the Jewish scum that murdered my sons. I want retribution. If it costs me my life, I don't care.' She paused briefly before continuing in a lower voice. 'With my sons dead, murdered by the Jewish soldiers, my life is worthless. I want to be a martyr for them, for their memory, and for absolution.' The determined look on her face left both men in no doubt about her resolve.

Henna kept the visit from the men to herself. She knew her husband would be angry at her for allowing strangers into their house with no family present. The next day, the stranger returned with the Imam from her local mosque. This time the Imam did the talking while the stranger studied her reactions.

'Henna, you are still grieving, still in shock, as we all are, at the loss of your two fine boys. They died an honourable death, and they assuredly have their place in paradise.' He gestured across to the stranger. 'What you said yesterday to my friend here is understandable, but what about your husband? If you take on a mission as a martyr, how will he cope without you?'

Without hesitation, Henna replied, 'Yes, there will be grief from my husband, but he has his job to help get him through this. He will understand and pray for me and our two boys when we will be together again.' She was resolute. 'I am determined to carry out my duty for my boys and for my country. I crave vengeance.'

* * *

In the aftermath of the battle, the IDF worked on tracking down the surviving Palestinian resistance to arrest them or kill them and bulldoze the family houses of known fighters and sympathisers. Three weeks after the end of the fighting, the doctor returned exhausted from a sixteen-hour shift at Nablus Hospital. He drove through his neighbourhood and turned into his street to find his house destroyed in a mound of rubble and his wife lying on the ground, sobbing inconsolably.

'Both our sons butchered by the Jews and now our house... our beautiful house has been destroyed by the Israeli scum.' The doctor saw his years of study and sacrifice crumble before his very eyes. After his family, the house had been his pride and joy. A sanctuary to return to and escape the pain and distress of hospital work with meagre resources and outdated equipment.

* * *

Henna Rafik attended daily prayers alone at her local mosque and two weeks after the visit from the Imam and the stranger, she was passed a note as she left. *Prepare for retribution. Come to the Hamas office and enter through the back door after Isha tomorrow.* Her heart skipped a few beats as she reread the message several times before it sank in. *Tomorrow night, I will begin my journey.* Time seemed to drag by slowly for Henna until the following evening. She was waved round to the back door by two heavily armed guards in dark-green army uniforms. The door opened as she approached and once inside, the stranger she had met previously again quizzed her on her determination to sacrifice herself and she reiterated her complete commitment.

'Next weekend is Passover. There is a feast at a hotel in the city of Natanya, north of Tel Aviv. This is where you will find justice for your murdered sons.' He led her into another room where a young woman dressed in the same green army uniform began instructing Henna on how to conceal the weapon she would wear on her day of retribution. She left the office and looked up into the night sky, smiling at what she took as an omen. A blood-red full moon shone down on Nablus.

One week later, the headlines in the Israeli newspapers screamed of the outrage felt by the Jews: *Twenty-one killed and one hundred and forty men and women seriously injured.* The story went into detail, noting that the explosion was so powerful only the suicide bomber's head remained intact. The article went on to say some of the victims had been survivors of the Holocaust only to be slaughtered by a female Palestinian suicide bomber dressed as a Jewish woman and pretending to join the feast of the Passover – a family day, much like the Jewish equivalent of the Christian Christmas Day.

Chapter Nine

The doctor and his remaining possession, a battered old suitcase of clothes donated by friends and neighbours, was driven north and crossed the border into Lebanon, another statistic in the Red Crescent lists, another refugee driven out of his homeland. An innocent casualty of a vicious war whose victims were justice, decency, and humanity, together with many slain men, women, and children. Home was now a canvas tent in the Burj el Barajneh refugee camp in the southern outskirts of Beirut, one of the most deprived square miles on earth and a breeding ground for radicalism. Freezing cold in winter and oppressively hot in the summer. Home to over 30,000 Palestinians driven out of their homeland by war, destruction, and desperation. The staggering birth rates in the camp led to domestic violence, prostitution, drug-taking, and suicide. Refugee camps were a fertile recruiting ground for militias, gangs, and terrorist organisations.

Doctor Rafik was welcomed with open arms by the overworked staff of the Red Crescent supervising the running of the camp. Red Crescent staff worked tirelessly to alleviate human suffering in the many refugee camps that had engulfed the region. Within his first week working at the makeshift hospital, he had performed surgery on nine patients and assisted in the birth of seven children but had also seen three children die of disease. His skills, taught at Cairo University and honed at Nablus Hospital, were standing him in good stead.

The Lebanese authorities were frequent visitors to the refugee camps and aware of the excellent work carried out by Doctor Ramzi Rafik. Several times they offered him a junior doctor's position at Beirut's main hospital, far below his qualifications and with a lower salary than he currently received from the Red Crescent at the refugee camp. He was fully committed to helping his fellow refugees and on each occasion, the doctor politely declined the offers.

* * *

Beirut's huge explosion and subsequent mass of casualties triggered an emergency call for all available help from medical staff throughout the country. The doctor had just finished an appendectomy when a Red Crescent nurse rushed into his changing room. 'Doctor, did you hear the explosion? Downtown Beirut has been destroyed and there are many casualties. They need you to head for the central hospital immediately. There's a taxi waiting for you at the front door.' Ramzi Rafik, like every single person in the area, had heard and felt the explosion and he knew instinctively that this was no ordinary bomb. He threw on his coat and grabbed his emergency bag.

Upon arrival at the Beirut Central Hospital, Doctor Rafik made his way past stretchers filled with bleeding and injured casualties of the explosion and resulting fires all over the dock area and city centre. The hospital corridors were jammed with wounded and suffering of all ages, men, women, and children. Senior doctors had the grim task of selecting the injured people who were most in need of life-saving treatment but who were also likely to survive and passing over victims who were beyond saving.

One of the administration staff noticed Doctor Rafik and called him over. 'Thank you for your swift response, doctor.' He pointed to two female paramedics in the corner who looked dazed and exhausted already. 'I need you to accompany this ambulance crew to the Seaview apartment block in central Beirut. The block was in the path of the main blast and there are many injuries from broken glass. We can collect the dead and dying later.' Doctor Rafik was uncomfortable with these orders but understood the need to prioritise when the facilities were overwhelmed.

The administrator introduced him to the two paramedics. 'Doctor Rafik will check each victim and select the ones to be treated at the scene or transported to hospital. His decision will be final, understood?'

Both paramedics gave a weary nod of their head and a cynical smile. 'Come on, let's play God again,' said the older woman. With that, they slugged down the last of their coffee and headed out towards their waiting ambulance, bracing themselves for the scenes of destruction. Their country had only just recovered from fifteen years of a vicious, bloody civil war which had left a large portion of the population mourning the dead and injured.

Threading a careful trail through the debris, the ambulance headed towards the once-luxury apartment block of Seaview. The doctor tried to make small talk with the paramedics on the journey, but it was obvious that they held him in low esteem. Bad enough that he was a Palestinian, but even worse that he was a resident of a refugee camp. For ordinary Lebanese, the camps of Palestinian and Syrian refugees were an unwelcome burden on the economy and infrastructure of this fragile country, trying to rebuild itself after civil war

The doctor ignored the rebuff from the paramedics and exited the ambulance as soon as it pulled up outside what was left of the Seaview apartment block. Several lifeless and bloodied bodies were laid out in the foyer, covered up with blankets or curtains.

'We'll start at the top floor and work our way down. The lower floors have been protected by the surrounding buildings, so follow me.' Rafik headed to the staircase and made his way up the steps, crunching through piles of broken glass and debris.

By the time he reached the top floor, sixteen storeys up, he was breathing hard and sweating profusely. The two paramedics were similar, even though they were half the age of the doctor. He tried the front door of an apartment and found it locked. One of the security guards had followed them up and had brought a huge sledgehammer for such a situation as this. He swung the hammer at the lock and after four hefty blows, the lock gave way, and a fifth blow took the safety chain clean off its mountings.

The security guard moved to the neighbour's door, ready to carry out a similar action if needed, while the medical team entered the apartment of Layla Barrack. The doctor entered first, followed by the paramedics. They checked each room as they made their way in and eventually found the apartment owner lying in the corner of the ravaged living room. All glass windows had been destroyed by the blast and the young woman had bled to death through the severe injuries caused by the flying glass. As the doctor knelt beside the motionless body, he felt for a pulse among the carnage. 'There's nothing we can do for her. Let's move next door.'

As the two paramedics nodded in agreement and turned to leave the room, Doctor Rafik turned to follow them but hesitated, as he noticed her computer screen was on but had frozen with the shock of the blast coming into the room. He moved closer and saw on the screen a blurred image of a man in the process of bending down to pick up what appeared to be two bags. What caught the doctor's eye was the scene where this had taken place. It was unmistakably Martyrs' Square, about half a mile from where they were now, and the scene of the recent well-publicised murder of a Saudi Arabian businessman and member of the Saudi royal family. The doctor noticed a memory stick had been inserted into the computer. He leaned over and removed the stick and saw the screen go blank. Slipping the memory stick into his pocket, he hurried to join the others next door where he began treating an older man who had been in his bathroom and missed the brunt of the blast.

* * *

For three weeks, the doctor, alongside teams of paramedics, sifted through the debris of houses and offices ruined by the dockside explosion. By this time, all injured people had been found and treated and the task in hand was the recovery of dead bodies – a desperate and depressing task that left the doctor numb, exhausted, and dejected each night he returned to his tent in the refugee camp. He eventually received news from a Beirut Hospital official that he was no longer needed and returned to his life as a refugee.

All through the rescue and recovery mission in downtown Beirut, the doctor had concentrated on the task in hand. The work had deflected him from the memory of the grievous loss of his wife and two sons. A loss that had left him empty of spirit and acutely aware of his loneliness. Sleep had been hard to come by. Thoughts turned to his future and the need to find better prospects away from the dismal life of a stateless refugee. The memory stick taken from the dead woman's computer had been burning a hole in his pocket. Something inside his head told him that this was no ordinary piece of film. This could be the key to him escaping his life as a displaced person, his passport out of the refugee camp, if handled properly.

* * *

After returning to the refugee camp, Ramzi Rafik managed to access a computer at the camp administration office and sat alone watching as the full video told the story of the execution of the Saudi prince. Towards the end of the ten-minute video, a full and clear picture of the killer had emerged as he stooped to collect two bags before departing the scene.

Rafik was determined to turn the film of the murder of the Saudi prince into hard cash and a passport out of the refugee camp. He walked past the gates of the Saudi Arabian embassy several times, circling the building situated in the heart of Beirut's diplomatic area of Hamra. The district was busy with cafés full of people taking coffee and cigarettes in the shade of the hot sun, arguing about politics, the economy, and the endless Palestinian problem. An anxious Doctor Rafik finally plucked up enough courage to approach one of the guards at the embassy gate.

'I want to see an official from the embassy. I have information about the Saudi Arabian prince who was murdered in Beirut last month.' The guard considered the request and rather than turn the stranger away with a warning to stop wasting his time, he telephoned the reception and passed on the message. After a full six- or seven-minute delay, the phone at the gate was answered by the guard and the stranger was shown inside with the instruction to ask for Maher Khatab.

Khatab had the title of Deputy Ambassador but everyone inside the Saudi embassy knew he was the Mabahith representative in Lebanon and wielded more power and influence inside the embassy than the ambassador himself. He had a reputation for violence and unrestrained brutality.

Ramzi Rafik had been smart enough to copy a small excerpt of the video onto another memory stick and leave the original behind, well hidden in a remote area of the refugee camp. At this stage, Rafik gave no details of who he was or where he'd obtained the video. He simply told Maher Khatab that he had found the full-length video in a damaged building when assisting with the search-and-rescue operation after the dockside explosion. Khatab looked at the footage many times before asking Rafik what the rest of the video showed.

'Mr Khatab, the film shows the murder of your royal prince and, more importantly, it shows the face of his killer.' Maher Khatab knew the Mabahith and the Saudi Arabian royal family were desperate to identify the killer and bring Saudi justice on him, preferably by public execution or the next best thing – death by any means possible.

Khatab fixed his steely stare on the doctor as he asked, 'How much will the complete film cost?'

Doctor Rafik paused, savouring the question, his heart pounding, before answering, 'As much as you think it's worth to you and your government. I'm a doctor and have no experience of this type of negotiation. However, I'm sure you will be fair and reasonable with your offer. We are both too busy to be haggling over money. I also have a duplicate copy which an associate will pass to the Americans in the event of me unexpectedly disappearing after we have completed our deal.'

Maher Khatab smiled, recognising the strength of the doctor's position. 'Please wait at the reception. I will order you coffee while I make a telephone call to see how we can progress this offer to our mutual satisfaction.'

* * *

'Ten million US dollars deposited in cash to a bank account of your choosing,' was the opening line from Maher Khatab after Ramzi Rafik had been invited back into his office. Rafik's head was spinning at the thought of such a sum of money as he forced himself to show no emotion at the offer.

'Mr Khatab, you and I know this is a priceless piece of evidence to help you in the hunt for the killer of the prince, so fifteen million US dollars and a Saudi passport will be sufficient to conclude the transaction to everyone's satisfaction.'

Maher Khatab rose from his seat and held out his hand. 'You are a very good negotiator, doctor, congratulations on securing a deal.'

Ramzi Rafik rose from his seat, smiling, and shook his hand. 'Rafik, Ramzi Rafik.'

The opening of a bank account in Miami, a new passport, and the application and issue of a visa for the United States of America took a matter of days. Doctor Rafik quickly found that cash greased the wheels of progress and things happened much faster than normal. Once the transfer had been completed, the handover of the memory stick containing the full video took place at the restaurant at the Crown Plaza Hotel in downtown Beirut. With both parties satisfied, Maher Khatab treated Doctor Rafik to a sumptuous lunch. Maher contemplated his reward from his employers for obtaining the video and Doctor Rafik thrust his chest out, tingling all over as he dreamed of a new life as an American citizen in the sunshine state of Florida.

PART III

Chapter Ten

The young woman pushed through the swing doors of the hotel entrance, struggling to drag her wheeled holdall behind her and weighed down by an overloaded backpack strapped onto her shoulders. She was closely followed by her boyfriend, who appeared to be travelling lighter, carrying only a holdall and an Oslo airport duty-free plastic carrier bag. They were both visibly relieved and grateful to have survived the half-hour white-knuckle taxi ride from the airport, weaving in and out of the speeding traffic of Beirut to the historical city of Sidon.

They were greeted by a well-trained young man at reception. 'Welcome to the Hotel Byblos, Sidon's finest five-star hotel. Please leave your bags and our porter will take care of them.'

The woman gave her boyfriend a weary smile as she turned to the receptionist. 'We have a reservation in the name of Olsen.' She reached into the inside pocket of her jacket and pulled out their passports.

The receptionist typed her name into the computer and the reservation showed on screen as a luxury suite booked for seven nights. Although surprised, he had been well trained not to show any reaction to people's looks and dress sense when they checked into one of the most expensive hotels in the Eastern Mediterranean. He scooped up both passports and handed them to his assistant with instruction in Arabic to photocopy the personal details and immigration entry stamps for both guests.

'Although your room has been prepaid, can I take a print of a credit card to cover any costs you might wish to charge to your room during your stay? This is just a formality required by the hotel.' Kari Olsen fished out her wallet and handed over her bank card. The receptionist could not hide his look of surprise. The plain black bank card had no logo or decorative picture, just the bank name, the account holder's name, and its unique number all in gold. During his time at the hotel, he had never seen a credit card like this.

Throughout the check-in process, Kari Olsen's boyfriend had stood back and let her handle everything. He looked around and admired the ambience of the lobby, the quality of the layout, and the unmistakable Middle Eastern architecture and interior design. Sven Solberg knew he had won the jackpot when Kari had asked him to accompany her on her gap year from Oslo University to go on a trip to visit the vestiges of the Roman Empire, one of the many armies that had conquered and occupied the Eastern Mediterranean region, once known as The Levant. Kari knew that the Eastern Mediterranean was rich in culture and resources and seen as the gateway to Asia. Her studies taught her that after many years of domination by the Turkish Ottoman Empire, the region was divided up by the British and French at the end of World War One. This caused an imperial hotchpotch that would sow political and religious conflicts for the next hundred years and was still felt in the region to this day.

* * *

Kari Olsen had an unmistakable Nordic look, with long straight blonde hair, sparkling blue eyes, perfect teeth, and a smile to match. Although she was dressed down for her travels, she could light up a room when she appeared in a designer dress and shoes emphasising her slim, tall body and athletic shape.

Kari had met Sven at Oslo University when she was in her first year studying History and he was in his second year of a three-year Petroleum Engineering course. Sven was tall, with good looks and, unusually for a Norwegian, dark brown, almost black hair. He came from a working-class family, from the city of Fredrikstad, in Southern Norway, close to the Swedish border. His mother and father knew that a degree in Petroleum Engineering would provide their son with a comfortable and secure living for the rest of his life, protected by the Norwegian jobs policy of putting locals first. His parents and sisters had never met Kari Olsen, but they had seen photographs on social media of this Norwegian beauty and were pleased with Sven's choice of girlfriend.

In truth, Kari had chosen him. She had confidently walked over to where he sat alone with a coffee, and her first ever words spoken to him had been 'We will sleep together tonight. I think you and I will get on well.'

Her forwardness was typical of today's young and self-assured Norwegian women, but Sven was still taken aback by her bold and presumptuous advance. She had the looks and the family background to have her pick of any of the eligible bachelors in the city of Oslo and she was fully aware of this. Kari had been born into a famous and wealthy family. Her great-grandfather Henrik Olsen had first made his fortune in the whaling industry before turning to fishing.

He had led the Norwegian resistance to German occupation during World War Two, escaping capture and certain death several times. At the end of the war, Henrik Olsen was recognised as a national hero and became firm friends of the Norwegian royal family.

When Kari's father, Johan, grew up and started his shipping business, he visited various members of the Norwegian government. Each one answered his request for work with a similar question: 'What do you need and when do you need it?' Olsen Shipping was rewarded with enough work to grow the business each year at an astounding rate and Johan soon became wealthy enough to be asked to join the board of the Norwegian government's fledgling sovereign wealth fund in 1990. It was set up to invest Norway's fast-growing oil and gas revenue. The financial project developed into the largest investment fund in the world, reputed to own shares in more than 9,000 industrial companies listed in more than seventy-five stock exchanges around the world. Norwegian public opinion demanded that the portfolio exclude companies involved in child labour, arms manufacture, environmental issues, or violations of human rights, and the fund management strictly applied these regulations.

* * *

Kari approached the young man on reception who had checked them in the previous day. 'We need to arrange a car and a driver for tomorrow to take us to Baalbek to visit the Roman temples. After yesterday's near-death experience with our taxi driver from the airport, I want somebody reliable and safe.' The receptionist smiled, reached under the counter, and produced a colourful leaflet for the Sidon Lux Taxi Company.

'Madam, this is the best private hire in all of Sidon. My cousin works there as a driver. I will personally request him to be your driver tomorrow.'

Kari gave the leaflet a quick scan and nodded in agreement. 'I know it's a long way away, so can he be here at eight o'clock tomorrow morning?'

The young receptionist could barely hide his joy as he beamed back at Kari. 'I guarantee he will be outside the hotel from seven o'clock tomorrow morning.'

Unknown to either of the young Norwegians, the receptionist had taken home a copy of Kari's passport details, including the page containing emergency contacts. That evening, he started searching through the internet to try and trace the person wealthy enough to own a special credit card and afford a suite at the Hotel Byblos. His internet search eventually revealed the source of her apparent well-heeled prosperity. As he read the story of her father's business success and affluence, he reached for his mobile phone and dialled a number in the town of Bar Kimm, deep in the Bekaa Valley.

The call was answered on the first ring. 'Al salaam alaikum, this is Marwan Farik from the Hotel Byblos in Sidon'. He paused to allow the person time to recognise the name before continuing, 'We have the daughter of a very rich Norwegian businessman staying at the hotel. I think you might be interested if she pays you a visit. I will keep you informed of her movements.'

The voice on the other end of the phone gave a blunt reply. 'Shukraan sadikee. You have done well. Let me know as soon as you have any more news.'

As the call ended abruptly, Marwan felt a mixture of fear and excitement. He had always been loyal to his Hezbollah roots, but this was his first occasion of direct involvement since he had left his hometown of Bar Kimm. He did not know the name of the man he had spoken to but knew he would be a man of power and influence within the Shi'a community scattered around the Bekaa Valley.

Marwan Farik never knew how he'd managed to obtain a job at the prestigious Hotel Byblos in Sidon. He hadn't applied for the job, but before he left to go to Sidon, his father told him, 'Friends have helped open doors for you. Friends that will be repaid sometime in the future.' His father had passed him a piece of paper with a telephone number.

'Learn your job, say nothing of your family roots or your hometown, and one day you will find an opportunity to return this help.'

* * *

Few people in Sidon took any notice of the two fair-skinned young Europeans visiting the remains of the Roman baths recently excavated in the centre of Sidon. Kari's expensive camera was in action all morning as she enthused to her boyfriend about the quality of the archaeological site still being worked on by a swarm of devoted students from Sidon University, supervised by a team of specialists from various institutes around Europe and America. Kari wandered round the site, chatting non-stop with the students and engaging in conversation with an older gentleman from America who turned out to be the site director. 'Who was the emperor at the time the baths were built?' 'Where did the building materials originate?' 'Where did the slave labour come from?' The director smiled at her enthusiasm and answered her as best he could.

As the morning wore on and the heat of the day intensified,

Sven's enthusiasm began to wane as thoughts turned to a cold beer around the hotel swimming pool – a beer that was also ten times cheaper than back home in Norway. Careful not to upset his girlfriend's obvious eagerness, he tentatively suggested a break for lunch, which was met with a wry smile from a face dripping in perspiration from a mixture of excitement and the midday heat now burning ferociously from a cloudless blue sky.

'Okay, Sven, a quick sandwich before we return, as I've been promised a guided tour of the artefacts recovered from the site. The director is going to open his workshop and show me what's been discovered. I am so excited, so let's grab a quick bite and a juice.'

Sven hid his disappointment with a wide smile and a hug. 'I know how much this means to you and this is what we came for.' *The cold beer will have to wait*, he thought.

She turned to him, wiping the beads of sweat from her forehead and sweeping her arm around the scene. 'This is great but wait until we get to Baalbek tomorrow. The project director here says he will call his colleague at Baalbek and arrange a personal tour for us. This is so exciting, and way more than I could have dreamed of.'

After a quick lunch the couple returned to the site and were treated to an extensive tour of the Roman baths and the many items recovered during the excavation. Late in the afternoon the couple returned to their hotel, bedraggled, exhausted, with Kari barely able to contain her enthusiasm for their first full day in Lebanon. 'Everyone is so nice and helpful. I can't believe some of the people's comments back home when we said we were going to Lebanon. Remember how many times they said *war zone*? Honestly, some of my friends are so negative.'

Chapter Eleven

Marwan had waited for a quiet time. In his job as hotel receptionist, the mornings were busy with guests checking out and afternoons busy with new arrivals checking in. The less hectic two hours in between gave him the opportunity to leave his desk on the excuse of a toilet break and go to his staff quarters at the back of the hotel. He dialled the same number in Bar Kimm.

'Salaam alaikum, this is Marwan again from Hotel Byblos in Sidon. I have more news on the Norwegian woman. She and her boyfriend will go to Baalbek tomorrow by private taxi. They leave here early morning, around eight o'clock, and the driver is my cousin Daoud, who is also from Bar Kimm.'

The voice at the other end of the line sounded friendlier as he replied. 'This is excellent news, sadikee. I know your cousin Daoud very well and he is a loyal recruit to our cause. I will handle arrangements from here.' With that, the call was terminated. Marwan stared at his mobile phone, wanting to add *Please, do not harm the girl.*

Saif Al-Jafri had cut the call. He considered Marwan Farik a loyal young Shi'a but lacking the hard edge necessary for survival in Lebanon's Bekaa Valley.

Every adult from the age of fourteen carried weapons and received military training and funding from the Iranian

Revolutionary Guard. The region was self-governing and operated outside the control of the Lebanese government in Beirut. There was an abundance of fresh water in the Bekaa Valley whereas Lebanon's surrounding neighbours had an abundance of oil and gas. The fertile soil provided superb growing conditions for cannabis and opium, as well as cereal crops and vegetables to feed the rest of a scarcely cultivated Lebanon. Agriculture was controlled by Hezbollah, the armed militant group of Shi'a Islam Muslims, trained and financed by Iran. Their social policies were targeted at the mass of impoverished civilians to provide housing, food, and education.

Saif Al-Jafri was the local commander of the Jihad Council, the military wing of Hezbollah in the Bar Kimm area. His lifelong commitment to Shi'a causes included volunteering to fight on the side of Bosnia Herzegovina in the Bosnian War and recently taking command of a Hezbollah brigade in the fight against ISIS in western Syria. He considered the information on the Norwegian woman, the daughter of an extremely rich businessman, a legitimate source of money to further the cause of Shi'a Islam.

Al-Jafri drove his battered Mercedes saloon north to the city of Zahlé, the regional capital of the Bekaa Valley. Approaching a villa on the outskirts of the city, he slowed down to allow the heavily armed guards to identify him before they lifted the barrier and waved him through, giving him access to the compound of the Jihad Council headquarters. His pace was brisk and his mood high as he skipped up the stairs and addressed the officer at the front desk.

'I must see Hassan as a matter of urgency. I am sorry I did not telephone ahead, but I have sensitive information, and you know how our telephone system is compromised by the Israelis these days.'

The officer rose to his feet. 'Wait and I will see if he is free.' He returned quickly and showed Al-Jafri into the office of Hassan Nasrallah, the head of the Jihad Council.

Al-Jafri entered the office and greeted his regional commander. 'Al salaam alaikum, I have news of an excellent opportunity to help finance our cause.' He had grabbed the attention of his commander with this simple statement, who gestured to the chair opposite him.

'Alaikum salaam, please be seated, my friend. Start at the beginning and leave nothing out.' Al-Jafri proceeded to tell the commander everything he knew of the young couple from Norway since receiving the call from his contact at the Hotel Byblos in Sidon.

'This is indeed a golden opportunity for Hezbollah. Your man in the Hotel Byblos has done well and he will be rewarded.' The commander pondered the situation before adding, 'As they are Norwegian nationals, I do not expect any interference from the Americans or the Israelis.'

* * *

The next day, as the car slowly made its way along the corniche in the early morning traffic, the taxi driver Daoud turned inland, away from the Mediterranean Sea glistening in the early morning sun. He kept up a constant chatter in Arabic and broken English, most of which the two Norwegians either didn't understand or chose to answer with a smile. As the sun rose and the day got hotter, both passengers dozed as the drive to Baalbek took them alongside a huge cedar forest before climbing up a long torturous road around Mount Lebanon, across a narrow bridge over a fast-flowing river, and into the Bekaa Valley.

As the taxi drove through the outskirts of the last village before the bustling tourist city of Baalbek, the driver turned into a side road leading to yet another cedar forest. The passengers were unaware of the manoeuvre until the taxi came to a sudden halt, faced by a pick-up truck parked sideways across the road as a roadblock. Before Kari and Sven could comprehend what was happening, the rear doors of the taxi were ripped open by heavily armed men carrying machine guns, who dragged the occupants from the taxi, shouting in French 'Dehors – dehors!'

The Norwegians were pushed against the car at gunpoint. A third man, who appeared to be in charge, returned his pistol to his pocket and produced two large nylon cable ties, gestured for them to hold out their hands, and proceeded to wrap them tightly around their wrists. He then produced two black hoods and fitted them over each of their heads, resulting in total black-out for both Norwegians as they were led to the pick-up truck and bundled into the back seat before they were driven off.

The suddenness and speed caused both to cry out in terror and confusion. So unexpected and rapid were the turn of events, it took a few minutes before either one spoke. Sven was the first to calm down and analyse what had happened. He tried to reach over and give Kari a reassuring touch before a guard slapped his arm back by his side. Sven shouted in Norwegian, 'Kari, it's just money they're after.'

Kari sobbed uncontrollably and could not reply. Sven persisted, trying to get her to calm down. 'Cash, watches, and mobile phones – that's what they'll be after. We'll be okay.'

The journey lasted about twenty minutes, but for Kari, it seemed like a lifetime. She was so disorientated and shocked and could not comprehend the nightmare that was taking place. As the pick-up came to a halt, Kari and Sven were led into some sort of building in silence. Sven was led into a room where his pockets were searched and his wallet, passport, and mobile phone taken before the hood was removed. Blinking in the sudden light, he saw that he was in a small windowless room with no furniture other than a single bed. An armed man gestured for him to sit on the bed as he slammed the door behind him, double-locked the door, and switched off the mobile phone, passing it to his colleague.

The man who appeared to be in charge pulled the hood from Kari's head and searched her, removing her wallet, passport, and mobile phone, which he immediately switched off. He looked at the tall blonde Norwegian before addressing her in English. 'You are now in the care of the guardians of this valley. If you comply with everything you are told, you will come to no harm.' He looked into Kari's eyes. 'Do you understand?'

A sobbing Kari was able to answer him. 'Where am I and what do you want with us? We're just tourists. Please don't harm us. We've done nothing wrong.' The group leader gave her a sardonic smile, showing a set of teeth that competed for space in his mouth.

'Miss Olsen, you are correct in saying you have done nothing wrong and as long as that remains the case, you and your boyfriend will be safe.' Kari gasped in shock at the mention of her name from a complete stranger. She was trying to comprehend this statement as she felt her legs give way and a rush of blood went to her head. She collapsed to the floor in the chaos and turmoil that had suddenly taken over her life. *How does he know my name? How did they know where we were?* she thought.

The leader dragged her to her feet. 'Give me the ring from your right hand.' Kari looked down at her hand in confusion. 'Take the ring off or I will cut off the finger with your ring on it.'

The menacing look from the leader left her in no doubt he would carry out his threat. She slid off the diamond ring given to her by her grandmother and handed it to the man. 'If your family value your life, you and the ring will be reunited. If your father tries to play games with us, you will never see the ring again.'

With that firm statement resounding in her ears, he took her photograph on his mobile phone before she was led away by the guard. The room she was led to was furnished with a single bed, a chair, and a small table with an empty plastic basin on it. The stark reality hit her and again she wondered how long this nightmare would go on for.

Chapter Twelve

When Johan Olsen never received his usual evening call from his daughter, he showed no concern. The previous evening, barely able to contain her excitement, she had told him of their plans to visit the Roman ruins of Baalbek, deep in the Lebanese countryside, and he presumed there had been trouble getting a mobile phone signal. Only after the third night of silence did he start to worry. He tried ringing both her and Sven's mobile phones only to be met with a dead ringtone on each occasion and his concern now turned into an uneasy apprehension.

His position as the head of the Norwegian Sovereign Fund gave him access to Norwegian government officials and a call to the foreign minister in Oslo got him a direct number to the man he needed to talk to. The second call he made was to the Norwegian embassy in Beirut, which left him even more distressed. After giving his name and his profession, he was immediately put through to the ambassador's personal line.

'I'm sorry to trouble you with something as trivial as this, but my daughter has not called for the past three days. I know you will say I am overreacting, but this is most unusual for her. I presume she had trouble getting a signal when in Baalbek.'

The ambassador immediately interrupted. 'Did you say Baalbek? In the heart of the Bekaa Valley? They travelled alone into one of the most dangerous parts of the world?' The ambassador could almost hear the sharp intake of breath on the other end of the line. 'Mr Olsen, we have a potentially serious problem here. Nobody should travel in the Bekaa Valley unescorted and certainly not someone of your family's wealth and prestige. Do you know which hotel she was staying at in Sidon?'

Johan Olsen was not a man who showed nerves or anxiety, but he was now unable to control the tremor in his voice. 'She and her boyfriend were staying at the Hotel Byblos. I booked it for her myself.'

Unseen at the other end of the line, the ambassador cradled his head in his left hand. He foresaw a huge problem before Olsen had spoken any more. Gently interrupting the troubled voice, he said, 'Mr Olsen, I do not wish to lecture you, but the Bekaa Valley is lawless. It's a stronghold of the radical Shi'a militia, Hezbollah, and virtually a self-governing state within Lebanon. These people are extremely dangerous, and it is now so dangerous it is a no-go area even for the Israeli army.'

'But what would they want with my daughter? A student who has no political opinions on the Middle East and is only interested in ancient Roman history. What harm could this cause to anyone?'

'Mr Olsen, you are in the business of buying and selling stocks and shares on the international market and by all accounts, you are very good at your job. The business in this region is more about selling commodities, items of high value... such as rich people and the daughters of rich people. The Western world calls it *kidnapping*; in the Bekaa Valley it's called *trading*. You pay me money and I will return your precious goods. This type of business has gone on for thousands of years.'

Johan Olsen was silent for a few moments, contemplating

this unexpected piece of news and devastated at the thought of his precious daughter being held for ransom. The ambassador paused before continuing. 'Mr Olsen, we have a very small diplomatic presence here in Lebanon and a skeleton staff to handle our business. We have no Norwegian military attaché or armed forces personnel. We do, however, work very closely with the British embassy, who have a much bigger staff here in Beirut.

'The military attaché Jeff Smith is a good friend as well as a fellow diplomat. I will have a discreet discussion with him to talk over our options.' The ambassador was about to end the call but added as an afterthought, as well as a warning, 'At this stage I don't know what options we have, but this may be a little clearer after I talk to the British.' The click ending the call left Johan Olsen feeling powerless and panic-stricken. His daughter was in serious trouble and there was nothing he could do but wait.

* * *

Five days of silence regarding his missing daughter was broken by the ring of his doorbell late in the evening. As he opened the door, he saw the taillights of a car disappearing down the driveway. A puzzled Johan Olsen looked down to see a small jiffy bag on the doorstep with his name handwritten in black pen. He sat down and looked over the package, seeing no other markings other than his name. His hands began to tremble as he tore open the package and cautiously opened the plain cardboard box to reveal a small golden ring and a handwritten note in English.

He glanced at the ring again but already knew exactly who it belonged to. His heart pounded as he carefully read the words on the note: *To see your daughter again you will transfer 2 million US dollars to the national bank in Tehran, to account no. 33947229. Any other action will result in her termination.*

This was a lot of money for most people, but not for a man of Johan Olsen's wealth. The next morning, he had his personal secretary arrange the transfer. She was used to carrying out his instructions without question and her loyalty and dedication had been unwavering since she had joined the company upon leaving college in Oslo.

Two days later another letter was left on his doorstep, addressed to him in the same handwriting. He expected to read instructions regarding the return of his daughter but was devastated to read the note. *The first payment was a deposit to confirm our position. The final payment will be an investment from your Sovereign Fund of 30 million US dollars in shares for the Mayak Group listed on the Lebanese stock market. Your daughter will then be returned unharmed to the Hotel Byblos.*

Johan Olsen sat back in his chair and placed both hands on his forehead, contemplating the horror of the situation. Never had he felt so alone since he'd lost his wife five years ago.

After a sleepless night going through various options and scenarios in his head, he showered and dressed and made his way to his office where he headed up the committee that ran the Norwegian government's ultra-successful Sovereign Fund. Johan Olsen knew that if he proposed buying shares in the Mayak Group, it would fail at the first hurdle. The Ethics Committee would throw it out based on the murky history of local Lebanese companies and their methods of securing contracts. Olsen had researched the Mayak Group and in particular Levi Mayak, the group founder. He was alleged to be the man behind the collapse of the electricity supply contract worth a reported $40 billion, paid by the Lebanese government for the construction of power plants which were later found to be inoperable and plunged many parts of Lebanon into permanent darkness.

Johan Olsen did something he would have never contemplated in the past and while he could not shake off his feelings of guilt, his love for his daughter overrode his conscience. He drew up a Sovereign Fund investment document for the purchase of $30 million worth of shares in the Mayak Group. He then took a previous investment document which had gone through the appropriate approvals and traced the signatures, before transferring them onto his new investment document. He placed the papers in a sealed envelope and instructed his personal secretary to deliver the document directly to the manager of Norway's national bank. She sat and sipped a strong cup of coffee in the bank manager's office while the transaction took place.

* * *

At the British embassy in Beirut, ex-Royal Navy officer Jeff Smith had been resident for just over a year after serving three years as assistant military attaché in Tehran. His promotion came after some excellent undercover work between the British and Iranian security services, working together to shut down funding to ISIS from Arabian Gulf states. The telephone call from Lars Newburg, the Norwegian ambassador, intrigued him as much as the choice of meeting place. The lift in the Allegro Hotel took him to the rooftop bar where Newburg sat waiting for him at a table in a faraway corner. Apart from the bartender, the place was deserted.

They shook hands and exchanged pleasantries and after a

quick check around to ensure they were out of earshot, the ambassador got straight down to business. 'My government has a potential problem on its hands – a problem that would have been avoided had the correct procedures been followed.' Lars Newburg paused then continued: 'The daughter of one of the richest men in Norway has disappeared in the Bekaa Valley. She and her boyfriend were heading for Baalbek but have been out of contact for more than four days now and we are extremely worried.' Newburg looked straight at Smith for his reaction and saw and heard what he feared.

Jeff Smith stared down at the floor, slowly shook his head, and mumbled, 'Jesus Christ, is there no end to some people's stupidity? What in hell's name made them go there? Has anyone made contact yet?'

Newburg shuffled uncomfortably in his seat and replied, 'No contact yet, but if she has been taken, then it's only a matter of time before we hear something. Do you have any idea where they would take her? Will they harm her?'

Smith looked him straight in the eye. 'She'll be alive for now. A dead body doesn't get much ransom money, but the longer this goes on, the more dangerous this will be for her. They will want to make as much money as they can before getting rid of the evidence or selling her on to some other radical group.' Jeff Smith's mind raced through various scenarios, none of them good. Going on past history, none had a good ending.

He needed somebody who could speak the language like an Arab and, most importantly, thought like an Arab. His mind went back to the MI6 agent who'd carried out a highly successful mission getting an Egyptian accountant out from under the noses of ISIS. 'I need to make a phone call. I'll meet you here this afternoon, say four o'clock?' They rose together and shook hands, the Norwegian full of worry and the Brit full of uncertainty.

Jeff Smith returned to the British embassy set on a hilltop overlooking Zaitunay Bay and hurried up the flight of stairs leading to his office. He picked up the secure phone and speed-dialled the number for Steve Foley, former head of the Middle East section and now chief of MI6. Smith had been a colleague of Foley and had worked with him in the past when posted to the British embassy in Tehran.

'Hi, Steve, thanks for taking the call so quickly. Our Norwegian friends have a problem, and they are asking us for help.'

As he explained the information passed on by the Norwegians, Foley wrinkled his nose and exhaled audibly in frustration and annoyance at the sheer stupidity of some people. 'Has there been any contact from the kidnappers yet?'

'No, nothing as yet. What do you think? Is Rory McAdam available?' came the tentative enquiry.

Chapter Thirteen

The phone call from the Norwegian prime minister, Anna Larsson, to 10 Downing Street was first answered by the prime minister's private secretary, the most senior civil servant in the country. The call was then transferred to the British prime minister, recently returned from Westminster Parliament. David Wallace took a deep breath and steeled himself. 'Good afternoon, Prime Minister Larsson. What can I do for you?'

There was a slight pause before the Norwegian prime minister replied. 'Prime Minister Wallace, I have just finished a conference between our head of armed forces, our ambassador to Lebanon, and our king. We are facing a serious problem over a kidnapping of two Norwegian citizens in Lebanon.' Anna Larsson let the initial piece of news digest before she continued. 'An initial demand was paid by the father of one of the kidnap victims. No release was forthcoming, and he faced a second demand to arrange the purchase of a large number of shares in a Lebanese construction company. The money has subsequently disappeared, and all the Norwegian Sovereign Fund is left with is a useless piece of paper for shares in a company of dubious ethics, and the kidnap victims are still being held.' Her voice tailed off in embarrassment at the decision-making of the man heading up the legendary Sovereign Fund.

The British prime minister listened with growing concern. 'Are the victims from a wealthy family?'

The Norwegian sighed audibly. 'Yes, the woman, Kari Olsen, is from one of the richest and most influential families in Norway. She's the only daughter of Johan Olsen, who owns a financial empire which includes a vast fleet of cargo ships, luxury cruise liners, a fleet of passenger aircraft, and a fleet of oil drilling rigs. As I'm sure you know, Johan Olsen also runs the Sovereign Fund on behalf of the Norwegian government.'

David Wallace let out a low whistle at the gravity of this news. 'And her father let her go to Lebanon without any close protection?' If he could have seen the Norwegian prime minister at this point, he would have witnessed her grimacing and curling her toes in frustration.

'Her father knows that this should never have happened, but we now have to find a solution to this dreadful business,' Anna Larsson said. 'This is why I am making this call. We desperately need the help of the British armed forces. We don't have the resources or experience to attempt a hostage rescue mission, but you and I both know that the British have an excellent reputation for this kind of undertaking.'

David Wallace was deep in thought at the news he just received when Prime Minister Larsson played her trump card. 'Of course, if you can help with this predicament we find ourselves in, I will immediately instruct our energy minister to cease any further negotiations with your Treasury Department and sign the long-term, cut-price gas-supply agreement that your government is seeking.'

David Wallace could not refrain from making an ironic smile. In politics, even in an extreme hostage situation, there was always some give and take, some bargaining chip to help smooth the decision-making process. This was a golden opportunity to seal a significant supply of much-needed energy, which on its own would probably be enough to secure his party another term in office at the next general election.

'Prime Minister Larsson, for an operation of this magnitude, the decision cannot be mine alone. I will need to consult with my specialists in this field. I understand the urgency of the situation and can promise you a speedy decision. I will call together a meeting tonight and telephone you as soon as we've reached a decision.'

With that they said their goodbyes with Anna Larsson a good deal more relieved than she had been fifteen minutes earlier and David Wallace a lot more concerned.

* * *

Phone calls from the British prime minister were made to the Director of Special Forces of the British Army, the Minister of Defence, the head of the Secret Intelligence Service MI6, and his counterpart in MI5. The briefing took place in the basement of 10 Downing Street, not the usual Cobra meeting room in Whitehall. Short lines of communication and a small team of specialists were needed to speed up the process. David Wallace passed round a written summary of the facts given by the Norwegian government and a hastily put together report from Jeff Smith in Lebanon on the situation in the Bekaa Valley and the area around Baalbek, where the kidnap victims were reported to have been heading.

Steve Foley, the head of MI6, also passed round a brief report prepared by his Middle East section chief on the current situation in Lebanon, specifically the Bekaa Valley. At the invitation of the prime minister, he opened the meeting with a stark reminder to the four others at the table. 'Even before the massive damage caused by the explosion at the Beirut docks, Lebanon was in chaos. The different groups vying for power and influence are run mainly by corrupt politicians and mafia-type leaders. Maronite Christians, Druze, White Russians, Armenians, Greek Orthodox, Syrians, and Palestinians all fight for domination in different areas of the country. There's also a huge refugee problem caused by various wars in neighbouring countries, resulting in refugees spilling over into Lebanon.' He looked around the table and saw he had everyone's full attention. David Wallace nodded for him to continue.

'The one exception to this continual fight for money and control are the Shi'a Muslims. They were originally some of the poorest and neglected groups of people in the country. But under the influence of Iran, the Shi'a population receive financial support and education, and the young men receive military training and weapons. This became the birth of Hezbollah, a paramilitary group that has evolved into a well-disciplined and powerful organisation,' Foley continued. 'Hezbollah dominate the south of Lebanon, particularly the Bekaa Valley. Every man, woman, and child are loyal to Hezbollah. Roadblocks are numerous and every boy over the age of twelve carries a weapon. This is not a place to be taken lightly or to go to underprepared.'

With that gloomy assessment completed, Steve Foley sat down, ready to take questions. They came at him thick and fast from Brigadier John Stevenson, the Director of Special Forces. 'Do you have any assets in the region?'

Foley answered, 'Yes, but not in the Bekaa Valley, only in other parts of Lebanon.'

Stevenson persisted. 'How about the Israelis or the Americans?'

Foley held up his left hand. 'I don't know, but I can try and find out.'

Satisfied, the brigadier turned to the prime minister. 'Can you make this a top priority? We have a specialist team in the region that could be redeployed, but we would need a detailed briefing before undertaking a mission as risky as this.'

The rest of the meeting was taken up by discussing a practical and realistic timescale, knowing that the Norwegians would like to move as soon as possible, and the clock was ticking. Brigadier Stevenson typed 'Bekaa Valley' into his computer and looked at the terrain in the area and the multitude of possible locations that could hide the kidnap victims. 'Looking for a needle in a haystack,' was heard several times around the table until a secure conference call was put through to the Beirut military attaché, Jeff Smith.

* * *

Smith briefed the group with an update of the situation. 'Earlier today I spoke with Johan Olsen. He told me he had booked them into the Hotel Byblos in Sidon under the name Olsen. He also told me he normally received a daily telephone call from his daughter on her mobile phone. Missed calls three days running sent alarm bells ringing and triggered the start of his nightmare. I've had a look around the Hotel Byblos and suspect that the information on who the woman is would have been passed on by one of the hotel staff who had access to the guests' booking and passport details. Four people share shifts on the front desk. A French woman who is a trainee, an older man who wears a crucifix, so is probably Christian, which leaves two possible men who set the kidnap in motion.'

Steve Foley spoke first. 'Great work, Jeff. Can you get any details on the two possible suspects at the front desk?' Smith paused before he replied, 'Its going to be very difficult but I can try and see what I can dig up'.

Next came Bruce Reid, the MI5 chief. 'Do we know who the Norwegian mobile phone network supplier is? We recently carried out a covert operation here in England where we tracked down the location of a terrorist who thought he was safe to move around London because he had his mobile phone switched off, secure in his backpack. With the help of the CIA, we were able to switch the phone on remotely using a system produced by the NSA in the States. It was enough to pinpoint his location and led to us intercepting a potential terror attack. This is obviously dependent on the phone being in the same location as the target, and hopefully it has not been smashed to pieces.'

Jeff Smith smiled to himself on the other end of the call, never surprised about the resources and ingenuity behind the fight against terrorists. 'I'll call Olsen and get the information for you.'

Brigadier Stevenson raised a further point for Jeff Smith. 'What about the taxi that took them to Baalbek? Can we get anything on the driver or the taxi company?'

Wilson raised his eyebrows in consternation. 'Sir, I'm the military attaché here and have only basic Arabic language skills. I would need some expert assistance to enable me to investigate the front-desk employees at the hotel and the taxi company. With respect, it will be time-consuming and may well lead to the perpetrators going to ground. I suggest we concentrate on the release of the hostages.'

There was silence, broken by the prime minister looking at each individual round the table. 'How fast can we get a plan and a hostage rescue team together?'

There was silence again, with nobody willing to commit until Steve Foley finally spoke. 'Rory McAdam is working in the region with an SAS team on Operation Babylon. I could get him and his team to you, hopefully by tomorrow. Jeff, I know you've worked successfully with Mac in the past.'

Foley then turned to the brigadier. 'John, you will be aware McAdam is leading the operation to track down former ISIS renegades in Northern Syria. It might be an idea to move the whole Babylon unit to Beirut so at least we have a team in place.'

Brigadier Stevenson gave Foley a broad smile. 'You read my mind. I was going to suggest that until you got in their first. The Babylon unit are all Arabic speakers and immersed in the Arabic way of life. Mac and his team look and sound more like Arabs than many genuine Arabs I have come across. With your permission, prime minister, I can temporarily halt Operation Babylon and move McAdam and the unit to Beirut where Jeff Smith can bring them up to date on the latest developments.'

The prime minister gave an immediate yes as he began to think of the economic boost of the gas-supply agreement with the Norwegians. He closed the meeting with an instruction to meet again, same place and time tomorrow evening. Before closing, he added, 'There's an open budget on this operation. There will be no delays in any expenditure approvals necessary to bring these hostages out safely.'

As they began to rise and depart, Steve Foley turned to the prime minister. 'If we could get some satellite and drone help from the Americans, it could help us locate the kidnappers and save a huge amount of time and effort.'

David Wallace nodded as he replied, 'Good shout, Steve. I'll call the president tonight.'

Chapter Fourteen

Rory McAdam peered through his military-issue binoculars as he concentrated on the seven men carrying Kalashnikovs and dressed in camouflage fatigues with black scarfs wrapped around their heads and covering most of their lower faces. They had parked their pick-up truck on the outskirts of Maaloula, a Christian town carved out of the Syrian mountains and studded with the domes of several churches. The seven men began advancing towards a single-storey house close to an ancient-looking church on the edge of the town.

Mac and the four SAS troopers were undertaking an operation, which involved the rescue of a Christian missionary. The man originally from Wales, had been a resident of Maaloula for the past nine years, living peacefully among the local Syrian Christians and learning the ancient Aramaic biblical language still spoken in the town.

The British foreign office had received reports of the missionary being threatened with death by crucifixion by a radical extremist group called Jaysh-Al-Islam, the army of Islam who had retreated from the Syrian region of Eastern Ghouta after heavy bombing by the Russians and Syrians leading to the fall of ISIS in this part of Syria.

The four SAS soldiers accompanying Mac observed the seven men through their binoculars from the rooftop cover of an abandoned and bomb-damaged school. The patrol sergeant Ross McDonald spoke softly to Mac without taking his eyes off his target. 'I have a positive ID on all suspects, members of Jaysh, and they are approaching the house occupied by Morgan Thomas.'

Mac's breathing become a little easier as he agreed with the troop sergeant. 'Thank God all this waiting and watching has finally paid off. I was beginning to think we had been sold a dummy.' Mac thought through the options before adding, 'Let's get closer and see if we can capture a prisoner. I am sure the local warlords will be able to extract some useful information, one way or another.'

Sergeant McDonald gave the signal as the SAS troopers fanned out and closed in on the seven men who were seen to kick down the door and disappear into the missionary's house. Mac stuck behind the troop leader, McDonald, to avoiding getting in the road of a well-rehearsed squad of specialists who approached the house using all cover that was available. Troopers Montgomery and Wilson split and went to the rear of the house, finding some large rocks to give them protection while covering the back door. Mac followed McDonald and Roberts to the front of the house where they observed the front door wide open and a Jaysh standing guard and cradling his AK47 across his chest. McDonald pressed the activator on his clip-on microphone and whispered to his troopers, 'One guarding the front door, presume six rags plus the padre inside.'

Wilson answered, 'Roger, boss, no one at the rear.' The sergeant knew speed was of the essence if they wanted to save the preacher.

'Moving in now, wait for the flash-bang to work.' Trooper Roberts raised his Heckler & Koch assault rifle with its stubby silencer fitted, took aim, and fired two bullets in a well-practised double tap with the first bullet entering the guard's chest followed immediately by another into his forehead.

McDonald loped forward to the open door and threw in two stun grenades, which produced a deafening bang and a blinding light, completely disorientating all the occupants in the house. The noise of the grenades was the signal for troopers Montgomery and Wilson to smash down the flimsy back door and enter what appeared to be a small kitchen.

McDonald, Roberts, and Mac burst through the front door and came across several bodies lying on the floor, stunned with the sudden loss of sight and hearing. Roberts moved to his right and kicked away the Kalashnikov of the terrorist nearest to him as the man lay moaning, with blood seeping out of his ears. McDonald had moved left and saw three men in a heap, semi-conscious and in a daze. Mac followed in behind McDonald and saw one of the terrorists begin to stir back to life before a burst from Mac's gun slapped him back to the ground, lifeless, and almost headless after the series of bullets nearly severed the man's head from his neck.

The two SAS troopers in the kitchen could hear the gunfire in the front room and cautiously opened the door to the scene of carnage, careful not to be mistaken for one of the terrorists. McDonald and Roberts saw the door open and signalled with raised fists that they recognised their colleagues. Five seconds after the stun grenades had exploded, their effects began to wear off and the bodies strewn about the floor began to groan in pain as they regained consciousness, temporally blinded and in acute pain from burst eardrums. Several men began to reach for their weapons only to be cut down by gunfire from the SAS troopers.

Roberts stood over the Jaysh soldier he had disarmed, grabbed him by the scruff of the neck, and dragged him outside, binding his hands and feet with cable ties. The Welsh missionary was in a state of shock with the suddenness of the arrival of hooded and heavily armed men of Jaysh-Al-Islam, swiftly followed by thunderous explosions and blinding lights. His confusion was now compounded by the appearance of a rescue party, which he could barely make out, nor could he hear a word that was spoken. He did know he was in safe hands as these strangers in army uniform, but with no identifying badges or markings, helped him to his feet and sat him down on a chair while his eyes adjusted. 'I don't know who you are, but thank you for saving my life,' gasped a very grateful Morgan Thomas. Mac smiled at the strong Welsh accent, still unmistakable after nine years in the mountains of Syria.

Mac spoke with Sergeant McDonald, and both agreed it was time to move out. The noise of the exploding stun grenades would have been heard across the small town and would soon attract the local warlords of Maaloula. Mac approached the missionary and, with a mixture of gestures and sign language, signalled for the Welshman to follow them as they made their way to retrieve their truck, hidden in the valley below.

Morgan Thomas understood the offer of rescue from the men who had saved him and was extremely grateful. However, he was adamant that he wanted to stay in Maaloula.

Mac and the SAS troopers needed to get moving and shook hands with Morgan Thomas, thinking he was either very brave or very foolish to remain here in the wilds of the Syrian mountains, possibly a target for another raid from Jaysh-Al-Islam. They made their way down the mountains and back to their transport home.

Mac and the SAS troop travelled slowly back to their base

500 miles away in Kurdish-held Iraq. Halfway through the journey, Mac heard his satellite phone crackle into life with an incoming call, 'Urgent message from the office at home, Mac. Brigadier Stevenson no less. He needs you and the team to go to Cyprus and then Beirut. There's an RAF transporter on its way from Cyprus to Erbil, so get ready to leave first thing tomorrow morning.'

Mac groaned at the thought of leaving early. He turned to his SAS teammates and broke the news to them. 'Sorry, guys, but we've been ordered to fly to Cyprus for a mission briefing and then on to Beirut. We're flying out tomorrow morning.' The news was met with a shrug of shoulders as they started to think about packing away kit, weapons, and essentials.

The briefing meeting took place in the basement of the RAF station in Akrotiri in the southern part of Cyprus. In a tense atmosphere, Brigadier John Stevenson, MI6 Chief Steve Foley, and his head of Middle East section brought the Babylon team of Rory McAdam and the four SAS troopers up to speed with the latest information. The brigadier opened the briefing, giving them details on the Norwegian kidnap victims and their movements since their arrival in Beirut, passing round photographs of them as he spoke.

'The American J-SOC have been very helpful on this operation. My opposite number in Washington repositioned a group of four RQ-4 Global Hawk reconnaissance drones for round-the-clock surveillance, equipped with the latest laser and heat-seeking technology. The optics aboard these drones will be able to see the colour of your eyes, even in total darkness, from a height of 60,000 feet.'

The brigadier turned to Steve Foley and gestured for him to continue. 'Gentlemen, we've had a lucky breakthrough, but we must move fast to capitalise on this. Last night, at around three in the morning, we were able to remotely activate the mobile phone belonging to the prisoner Kari Olsen. This gave us enough time to pinpoint the location of the phone to a remote house west of Baalbek, high on a hill surrounded by a cedar forest. Although this area is remote, there are several houses and farms in the surrounding areas. These may well be occupied by Hezbollah soldiers or sympathisers.'

Foley let the team digest this information. 'The Americans were then able to adjust the position of their drone and confirm that there are eight human occupants in the house giving off heat signatures. This drone is so powerful that it can listen to individuals speaking to each other and even speaking on a mobile phone.

'The drone has picked up a woman's voice asking to use the toilet. This has since been analysed by the Americans and confirmed as the voice of Kari Olsen. She has also been picked up several times pleading with her kidnappers for information on the whereabouts and condition of her boyfriend, Sven Solberg. All requests by her have been aggressively rebuffed and there is growing concern about his safety.'

SAS Trooper Charlie Montgomery was the first to raise a question. 'Is the mobile phone still switched on?'

Brigadier Stevenson answered, 'No, we couldn't risk leaving it on in case the kidnappers saw it blinking and changed their location. As far as we know, they are completely unaware that we have found them and located the house where they're holding the hostages. The phone was live long enough to allow us to pinpoint the grid reference before it was switched off again.'

A stream of questions followed from Rory and the SAS troopers about the terrain around the house, guards and roadblocks in the vicinity, insertion and extraction plans, and transport options.

The SAS troop was made up of specialists in their own field. Tommy Roberts, nicknamed Worzel Gummidge on account of his strong Gloucester accent, was the troop's communications specialist. There was not much Tommy could not do with a radio, mobile phone, or computer. He was forever getting stick from his fellow troopers for being a tech geek. Born of mixed parentage with a Sudanese mother and an English father, Tommy was a six-foot-seven giant with film-star looks, and off duty in the pub he was known as the 'babe magnet'.

Scotsman Garry Wilson was the explosives expert and could make or defuse almost any bomb they were likely to encounter in the field. Garry loved his football and unusually for a southwest of Scotland boy, he chose to support Saint Mirren over the two Glasgow giants. This gave his friends a little insight to his character, unconventional and very individualistic.

The third member of the troop was cockney Charlie Montgomery, usually referred to by his mates as 'the Cockney Rebel' or 'Champagne Charlie', although nobody had ever seen him drink anything except beer – the darker the better according to Montgomery. He was the transport man and claimed he could drive any vehicle known to man from a moped to an articulated lorry. He could also repair most motorbikes, tanks, cars, or trucks and many times on operations had saved the troop a long walk home when their transport had broken down. His fellow troopers ribbed him about his expertise in hot-wiring cars as a sign of his misspent youth and his early days as a car thief.

The last member was the SAS troop leader, Sergeant Ross McDonald, who originally hailed from the Isle of Skye in the north-west of Scotland. McDonald was the oldest member of the troop at thirty-three and had served two previous tours with the SAS, seeing action in Afghanistan, Iraq, and, most recently, Syria. McDonald was the medical specialist and the link man between the troops and Rory McAdam.

They got on well, not just because both were Scots, but because there was a great affinity between them. McAdam was around the same age and both men had young families, but both were dedicated to their jobs and willing to put their lives on the line.

Now that the location of the kidnappers and their hostages was known, planning turned to insertion and extraction, and trying to avoid a gun battle. Mac and the SAS troopers were aware of the capabilities and reputation of the Hezbollah fighters, and this generated a lot of discussion on the methods they could use to enter and leave the Bekaa Valley unseen with the two hostages alive. Brigadier Stevenson's mobile phone buzzed.

He listened intently as the J-SOC commander relayed the information received from the military research centre in Virginia. 'We know the circumstances you're dealing with, in a very hostile environment, and I know you want to avoid a firefight at all costs. We may have a solution for you, based on the extensive photographs taken by our Global Hawk drone cameras.'

Brigadier Stevenson's pulse quickened at the thought of some good news. 'We know it's a relatively small house the kidnappers are using, and we also know that due to the high summer temperatures and humidity levels, they're using air-conditioning. Our drone has analysed the outside temperature and humidity levels and compared them with the levels inside the house. The significant difference is down to the use of air-conditioning.'

The J-SOC commander checked his written notes before continuing. 'Our specialist team have received information from a Russian asset inside the Russian Federal Security Service about an anaesthetic gas they used on Chechen rebels during the Moscow theatre siege a few years ago.'

Brigadier Stevenson interrupted. 'But the gas they used killed more hostages than they rescued.'

The J-SOC commander remained patient. 'Yes, Brigadier, we are well aware of that. However, we also received information on the chemical make-up of the gas from the CIA asset in Moscow and for the past ten years, we have been able to modify the chemical formula to make it less lethal but still an effective knock-out gas. We think this would be an ideal entry method to enable you to rescue the hostages without provoking World War Three.'

Brigadier Stevenson agreed that this could definitely be an option but needed to know more. 'How do we transport the gas to the location? How much will we need? And how far away is your supply of this gas?'

The J-SOC commander had anticipated these questions and was ready with his answers. 'You will need around twenty cubic metres to neutralise all occupants in a house of this size. This can be carried in standard gas cylinders that scuba divers use, which can be carried on the backs of your men and still give them enough manoeuvrability to operate.' The J-SOC commander let the brigadier absorb this latest piece of information before he concluded. 'We have a batch of this gas on route as we speak. It will be landing tonight on our aircraft carrier USS *Lexington* based in the Eastern Mediterranean. You have permission from our president to use the ship as your base for the rescue.'

Brigadier John Stevenson was about to end the transatlantic call with his opposite number in America when he began to think about adding some extra incentive for the American J-SOC to assist the operation.

'Commander, I think you and the president should be aware that the team leader on the ground is someone you will both be familiar with.' The J-SOC commander waited in expectation. 'Major Rory McAdam, holder of your government's highest honour, the Congressional Medal of Honour. Your assistance is greatly appreciated by all concerned.'

Unusually, the J-SOC commander was caught off guard momentarily. 'Brigadier, I'm sure glad you mentioned it. I will personally pass this on to the president. Let me know if there's anything else we can do to assist you, especially as it involves Major McAdam. His bravery is legendary inside the Pentagon and the White House.'

* * *

It was Ross McDonald who addressed the brigadier as he re-entered the room. 'Boss, we're looking at a HALO insertion to get to the target. The field identified in the satellite transmissions looks suitable and is not too far from the target house. We've all discussed it and agreed High Altitude, Low Opening is the way to the target and offers a lower risk of discovery.'

The brigadier nodded his satisfaction at this progress before adding, 'Okay, Ross, that's the way in. What about extraction with the hostages?'

'What the hell is an E-VTOL?' was the group response when Charlie first mentioned it.

'It's basically a stealth helicopter that the Americans are

developing. It's electric, so nearly silent in flight. They've been testing it for the last two years.' After a few minutes searching on his mobile phone, Charlie Montgomery passed round a picture of an aeroplane with four electric turbofans with blades pointed up to the sky. He had their attention now and could barely contain himself. 'Think of it as an electric helicopter. It takes off and lands silently with the blades pointed up and when clear of the ground, it tilts the engines back to horizontal and flies like a conventional aircraft. Well, that's what I read in a magazine.'

There was a stunned silence among the group of people before a buzz of conversation broke out with a stream of questions about how long development would take, was it even in production, would the Americans risk it in a live operation?

Brigadier Stevenson held up his hand to call for order. 'Gentlemen, the only way we can get answers to these questions is to ask the Americans. Let me make a call to start the ball rolling. In the meantime, continue to look at options to extract from the area. This E-VTOL, as you call it, is a long shot, so we need to keep planning an alternative.'

The brigadier left the room and placed a call on a direct line to Downing Street. Although it was late in the evening, David Wallace was in his office preparing for his speech to the CBI when his direct line rang.

'Apologies for the lateness of the call, Prime Minister, but you know our situation is time critical.'

David Wallace looked at his watch before replying, 'Brigadier, you have an open line to this office twenty-four hours a day. How can I help?'

Stevenson began to explain the dilemma they faced with extracting the hostages without encountering any of the militia groups located all over the valley. 'One of our men mentioned an electric-powered helicopter the Americans have developed. It's called an E-VTOL and would be ideal to lift the team and the hostages out of the valley without starting a firefight with Hezbollah and sustaining serious casualties.' The brigadier paused to let the prime minister absorb this information. 'Would you consider requesting assistance from the American president? I think only he could make this happen as the American Air Force will be reluctant to take a prototype into a live operation, especially into the Bekaa Valley.'

Prime Minister Wallace considered the request and expressed doubt that the Americans would risk such a sensitive piece of equipment in a hostile area in the Middle East. The brigadier had anticipated such a response and played his trump card. 'When you make the request to the president, remind him that Major Rory McAdam is leading the team on the ground and that the request for the E-VTOL has come directly from him.'

David Wallace broke into a broad smile. 'John, you certainly know how to put pressure on the man. You should have gone into politics. I'll make the call right now.'

* * *

Thirty minutes after Prime Minister David Wallace had spoken to the American president, the wheels were in motion to load the E-VTOL aircraft, now christened 'Skylark', aboard a Lockheed Super-Galaxy transporter plane from its base in Tennessee to the US airbase in Sicily. A team of technicians, as well as the chief test pilot, Captain Kris Evans, accompanied the Skylark on its long flight to Europe.

While the Skylark team were in transit to Sicily, the J-SOC commander appointed Colonel John Jamieson as the liaison between the Americans and the British, with overall operational command on all aspects of the rescue mission with American involvement. After being briefed on the planned insertion and extraction plan by Brigadier Stevenson, both Colonel Jamieson and the brigadier studied the drone footage and agreed on the only suitable landing site within striking distance of the target house – a field at the edge of a cedar forest that had a clearing large enough for the Skylark to land on, the same landing area that Mac and the SAS team would use when parachuting into the Bekaa Valley.

Chapter Fifteen

Confined inside the house on a diet of mainly flatbread, rice, and vegetables, Kari Olsen was desperate for freedom. Several times she had made futile attempts to run for the back door while going to the toilet and each time she had found her way barred by one of the guards.

Her boyfriend had also reached the point of desperation and saw his opportunity as one of the guards started a conversation with another guard while Sven came out of the toilet. Catching them off guard, Sven lunged forward and hit a guard with the full impact of his shoulder, knocking him forwards into the other, throwing both guards to the floor. Sven didn't hesitate and bolted through the front door, taking his first gulp of hot, dusty fresh air as he fled downhill towards the distant line of trees, his heart racing, his knees pounding. Ahead he could see the cedar forest rising to meet him, giving him hope of protection and a place to hide.

A muffled cry from behind told him that the guards were back on their feet. He pushed harder, adrenalin coursing through his limbs as he summoned every ounce of energy, desperate to reach the safety of the treeline. Sven heard the crack of the first shot and the bullet whistled past his head before ricocheting off a stone. The trees were almost in reach, the scent of pine resin drifting in the wind. *Just another few seconds*, he thought, trying to zig-zag and make himself a difficult target. Another crack of gunfire and a sharp searing pain told him his luck had ran out. The second bullet caught Sven Solberg high up on his left thigh. His leg crumpled beneath him, and he crashed to the ground in agony.

Turning to the confused group leader, the gunman shrugged his shoulders. 'I had no option. He was making a run for it.'

The look of disgust from his commander was unmistakable as he started issuing orders, first pointing to the guard who shot Sven. 'Call the doctor from Zahlé. Tell him it's an emergency and he will be treating a gunshot wound in the upper leg.' Turning to the three remaining guards, he added, 'You three, carry him inside and lie him on his bed. If the girl asks about the shots, tell her it was a hunter.' With that, he went back inside the house to make an uncomfortable call to the Hezbollah commander in Zahlé.

The doctor sweated profusely as he bent over his distressed patient and performed an emergency operation to remove the bullet lodged in Sven's femur, his assistant trying his best to stem the blood flow and keep the area around the wound clean and sterile. With no general anaesthetic available, the doctor had given Sven a local pain-killing injection as he tried to remove the bullet as quickly and cleanly as possible. No information had been given to the doctor as to the cause of injury and he knew better than to ask the question. This was the Bekaa Valley, and gunshot injuries were not uncommon.

Kari Olsen sat on her single bed two doors along the corridor in complete ignorance of the events taking place around her. She had become frantic when she heard the two gunshots and banged her fists on her door, shouting for the guards to tell her what was going on. 'A deer hunter' was the gruff answer she received before she was pushed back, and the door was slammed in her face and locked again.

* * *

The shooting incident and the subsequent discussions and phone calls by the kidnappers had been picked up by the Global Hawk drone circulating silently and invisibly, high above the location. These were seen and heard in real time in the operational headquarters in Cyprus, as well as inside the Pentagon 6,000 miles away, and had the immediate effect of speeding up the timetable for the hostage rescue. Experience had taught the special operations commanders that injuries to the hostages usually caused panic and hysteria, leading to irrational decision-making by the kidnappers.

Rory McAdam and the SAS team were already aboard USS *Lexington* cruising in the Eastern Mediterranean. Mac and the rest of the SAS team listened intently to the technical briefing on the gas they would use to neutralise the occupants of the house. 'As there are only five of you, the amount of gas you can carry will be at the operational limit for a house of this size with eight occupants.' There were nods of understanding from the five men listening intently. 'Once you reach the rear of the house, you will need to locate the compressor and disconnect the air hose connecting the air-conditioning unit to the house. Fit the gas manifold to the air hose and seal it airtight using these rolls of sealing tape.' Again, there were nods of understanding all round. 'While this is being done, the second man should be linking up the gas cylinders, ready to go into action.'

The HALO suits they would need to deploy were fitted with an electrical heating system and an oxygen tank, as well as a huge French-made B2-80 parachute designed to break their free fall from 120 mph to near zero in a matter of seconds. Each man packed his own kit consisting of an AR-15 assault rifle and spare ammunition, a Browning thirteen-shot pistol with silencer, a K-BAR knife, a medical pack, and a PRC-2 radio set.

Rory McAdam felt tense as he donned his suit, gloves, and boots. He had qualified as a HALO trooper during his time serving with the parachute regiment but had not jumped since receiving the bullet wounds in his ankle while serving in Afghanistan two years before. The wound was so severe that amputation of his lower left leg had been a real possibility at one stage of his hospital treatment. The injury had been serious enough to force him into accepting a medical discharge from the army before being recruited by British intelligence MI6. He prayed that his rebuilt ankle would be strong enough to withstand the heavy landing, especially with the extra kit they were carrying.

With a parachute plus reserve, kit bag, oxygen tank, and two cylinders of knock-out gas, and wearing NVG goggles, they looked more like astronauts than a hostage rescue team. They were unable to deploy body armour due to the already excessive load and bulk of their kit. Each of the five men needed assistance as they waddled aboard the American Air Force C-2 Greyhound aircraft. 'Dope on a rope, right enough,' quipped Trooper Wilson. To accommodate the unusual cargo of five parachuting troops, the aircraft had been stripped down of all surveillance equipment to make room for the men and lighten the load for take-off from the aircraft carrier as midnight approached.

* * *

In the American Air Force base in Sicily, Captain Kris Evans watched on as the Skylark was slowly unloaded from the transport plane, and the wings folded back and locked into place. He had managed a few hours of sleep on the flight over but could not stifle a yawn as he adjusted his watch to the six-hour time difference between Tennessee and Southern Europe. Kris looked up to the clear late-afternoon skies and pondered what was ahead. He had received a full briefing from Colonel Jamieson before departing his home airfield and was taken aback when given the news that there would be no room for his co-pilot, who had accompanied him on every test flight since the inaugural take-off. 'Sorry, Kris, we need to make room for the extraction team and the hostages. Steve will accompany you as far as the carrier as back-up, but we need all the space we can get to take the rescue team of five, plus the two hostages.' His immediate thoughts were, *Christ, the first combat mission into a hot landing zone and no co-pilot. Nothing's ever easy in this business.*

The electronic warfare team aboard the USS *Lexington* had briefed the pilot of the C-2 Greyhound and the rescue team, as well as Captain Evans aboard the Skylark.

'All radar, GPS, and radio signals will be jammed just before you enter Lebanese airspace. You will have to switch to the predetermined ultra-high frequency to activate your navigation system. The drone commander will communicate directly with both pilots, as well as the British commander on the ground. The troops will parachute into the landing zone and secure the ground at 0230. When the first phase of the mission is complete, they will signal the Skylark to come in for the extraction. Any questions, gentlemen?'

Captain Evans asked about the estimated time the rescue would take. 'The estimates vary between one and three hours, so plan on it being somewhere in between. Anything longer than that means the team is in trouble.'

* * *

The C-2 Greyhound took off from the USS *Lexington* at exactly two o'clock in the morning in total darkness and climbed rapidly through the cloud cover to an altitude of 30,000 feet where the sky was bathed in pale moonlight. Inside the aeroplane was total darkness and silence due to the high-altitude helmets worn by the paratroopers. Mac and his SAS troopers had piled on fleece-lined clothes, leggings, gloves, and socks to keep warm during the rapid free fall when they would experience windchill temperatures that could freeze a person to death.

As the pilot, guided by his ultra-high-frequency GPS, crossed into Lebanese airspace on a pre-set bearing, he felt comfortable in the knowledge that he was invisible to any standard radar tracking system. The few Lebanese air-force radar operators on duty that night had been looking at a blank screen for the past hour and presumed that the Israeli Air Force was responsible, as they had been on many previous occasions.

The Greyhound pilot gave the team a ten-minute warning to target. Mac signalled to the four troopers to get set to exit by the cargo door. Two minutes from target the door was opened, causing an icy blast of air to rapidly chill the inside of the aeroplane.

As the green light came on, Sergeant Ross McDonald flipped his NV goggles into place and dived out into the night sky, closely followed by the three other SAS troopers with Mac the last out of the aircraft. They plummeted at a staggering speed of 120 mph, which gave them a descent speed of 1,000 feet every five seconds.

Mac was overcome with a growing sense of dread as he jumped out of the aircraft. His suspect ankle, held together with a series of steel pins, was about to get a severe test upon impact. He forced himself to fully focus on the descent as the visor on his NV goggles began to freeze up, making it difficult to see the readings on his altimeter and compass. He quickly made up his mind to concentrate on the nearest trooper below and follow him all the way down to the landing zone.

His parachute was set to open automatically at 3,500 feet and as the opening device activated, Mac felt the huge parachute billow above him as his speed rapidly reduced and he was wrenched upwards. Mac looked up to check the chute had fully opened and gave silent thanks to the person who had packed the parachute. He remembered his training instructors ramming home to him time and time again: *It's not the free fall that kills you – it's the ground when you hit it.*

McDonald landed first, almost exactly where he wanted to be, in the middle of the field identified by the drone surveillance. As he struggled to remove his parachute and kit bag, he looked up to see the remaining four men coming in at staggered heights, landing safely in the field.

Mac, the last one to arrive, made a hard, clean landing, but the jarring impact caused acute pain in his damaged ankle. He dragged himself to his feet and limped over to join his teammates as they gathered up the chutes, HALO suits, oxygen tanks, and helmets. The parachute equipment was bundled up and hidden among a clump of cedar trees. No words were spoken as hand signals were used to spread the troopers around the field to check that they were alone and their insertion into the Bekaa Valley had gone unseen.

Satisfied that there was nobody in the vicinity, with Sergeant McDonald receiving constant feedback on the ground situation from the American drone operators, the team worked their way towards the hostage house, stopping every ten seconds to listen for any movement or barking dogs. They constantly scanned their surroundings through their NV goggles, which gave the whole area an eerie fog-green glow, magnifying the natural light thrown off by the moon and the stars. Within a range of 200 yards, any warm-blooded creature, including humans, would show up as a glowing thermal image on the visor of the NV goggles.

As they approached the house, Ross McDonald, taking operational command of the team on the ground, signalled for troopers Montgomery and Wilson to circle the house and check for any guards posted outside. Each SAS trooper carried an AR-15 assault rifle and a silenced 9mm Browning pistol. If they encountered guards or dogs, the silenced pistols would be used to take them down. The two-man patrol completed their circuit of the grounds and confirmed that there were no guards or dogs outside.

McDonald signalled for Montgomery and Roberts to go forward towards the central air-conditioning unit which the American drone had pinpointed at the rear of the house. Sergeant McDonald and Mac spread out and kept a watch on the front of the house.

As Montgomery and Roberts approached the air-conditioning unit, they heard the whirring of the fan circulating chilled air around the house, reducing the humidity to zero and keeping the inside temperature bearable. Both troopers lifted their NV goggles and blinked as their eyes adjusted to the natural light.

Charlie Montgomery dropped his rucksack to the ground and fished out a flexible hose that had been designed using drone pictures scaled up to show the approximate size of the unit's air intake. Monty slipped the oversized hose around the perimeter of the intake and held it in place as Roberts took out a roll of gaffer tape and wrapped it around the air intake, sealing it off. Trooper Roberts then added another two strips of tape around the intake to give some extra support to the hose connection.

Both men were relieved to be free of the heavy load they had carried on their back as they rigged up the gas cylinders to the manifold at the other end of the hose. After double-checking all connections, they opened both valves, satisfied that the gas was now being pumped throughout the house. As they watched the pressure gauge on the gas cylinders begin to drop, Roberts crept back over to his sergeant and indicated for the remainder of the gas cylinders to be taken over to Montgomery so he could swap them out as each cylinder emptied. The operation to pump all eight cylinders of gas into the house took just over two hours before the last cylinder gauge showed empty.

Sergeant McDonald signalled for everyone to put on their own gas mask as they crept forward, guns at the ready. McDonald tried the door handle but as expected, found it locked. He signalled for Wilson, the explosives expert, to come forward. He slid his gas mask up, looked carefully at the door lock, and checked the construction material and design of the door and lock before he reached into his rucksack and withdrew a small package wrapped in greaseproof paper. He pulled a small chunk off the main roll and shaped it in the palm of his hand so that it slotted into the keyhole of the lock. He rewrapped the package and returned it to his rucksack then extracted a small electronic detonator, which he slid into the putty-like substance that filled the keyhole. He returned to McDonald and gave him the thumbs up as he took out a small electronic device and keyed in a code number before he looked up and received a final nod from his sergeant.

Wilson lowered his gas mask into place and hit the green button on his device, creating a barely audible thud as the explosive blew the lock off the door. The troopers and a badly limping Mac followed Sergeant McDonald into the darkened building, using powerful torches fixed to the underside of their assault rifles to light up a path. As they entered the ground floor, they found one of the kidnappers in the hallway, lying unconscious from inhaling the knock-out gas. Montgomery reached into his pocket and pulled out heavy duty cable ties, which he used to tie the hands and feet of the unconscious man.

After clearing the ground floor and ensuring there were no other kidnappers or hostages, McDonald led the men upstairs and saw four doors, two on either side of the corridor. The first door he opened revealed two more kidnappers, still holding on to their Kalashnikovs but unconscious, one on a bed and the second one lying spreadeagled on the floor. Trooper Montgomery dealt with both men and quickly bound their hands and feet with cable ties.

Mac tried the second door and found it was open. As he entered and shone his torch towards the bed, he recognised the male hostage, Sven Solberg. Mac was shocked to see a huge blood-stained bandage around the hostage's left leg and the two intravenous drips connected to the back of each hand. Sitting on a chair next to the bed was an older man with glasses on. Surprisingly, the man was fully awake and sat upright on the chair. Mac then glanced to his right and saw that the window was open, allowing any gas to vent to the atmosphere.

Before Mac could speak, the man held up both hands, palms outward and speaking in Arabic. He addressed Mac in a very nervous tone. 'I am a civilian doctor brought in by these people to treat the wounded European boy. I am a Druze, not part of the Hezbollah.'

Mac started to reply in Arabic before switching to English. 'I'm not here to harm you. We're here to take the hostage's home. Where are they keeping the woman?'

The doctor had a look of relief as he answered Mac in English. 'She's in the room next to the boy I have been looking after. If you move the boy, you must keep giving him the antibiotics and pain relief I'm administering through the intravenous drips.'

Mac nodded and turned to McDonald, who had entered the room, surprised to hear Mac conversing with a man who should have been unconscious. He explained: 'He's the doctor who's been looking after the injured boy. He says he does not like air-conditioning and that's why he's still awake, as his unit wasn't switched on and the window is wide open. We should still tie him up but be gentle with him. He's no threat to us.'

Ross McDonald turned his attention to the locked door and asked Roberts to kick down the door. One kick was enough to shatter the flimsy lock as the door crashed open. A burst of automatic fire from inside the room sent Roberts crashing backwards with his chest ripped open by the gunman's bullets.

McDonald dived flat onto the corridor floor, raising his gun and firing a double tap into the room towards the source of the gunfire. The first bullet narrowly missed, but the second bullet caught the gunman in the groin, sending him down screaming in agony. McDonald got to his feet, cautiously entered the room, and noticed the blonde woman lying unconscious on top of a single bed. The SAS sergeant walked over to the gunman lying in a pool of blood and groaning in agony. He raised his gun and put a bullet into his forehead, quickly ending the dying man's torment.

Mac and Wilson were crouching over the body of Roberts, checking in vain for any signs of life. The burst of bullets into his chest had torn into his vital organs, hitting his lungs and heart, resulting in instant death. Montgomery joined them and looked in disbelief at the body of his friend. 'Five fucking years we've been together, in Afghanistan and Syria. We've been like brothers, and it ends like this!'

Monty and Wilson were having trouble holding it together until Sergeant McDonald joined them in the corridor. 'We are not leaving him behind. He comes back with us along with the hostages.'

McDonald checked his watch and turned to Mac. 'We need to get the two of them down to the landing zone while I ask for the Skylark to come in. If you carry the woman, Monty and Wilson will take the wounded lad. I will carry Roberts' body back with me.'

Mac nodded in agreement, hoping his damaged ankle would take the extra strain, then he bent down and picked up the limp body of Kari Olsen. Monty and Wilson lay a sheet on the floor, unhooked the drips, and eased Sven Solberg onto the sheet as he groaned in agony.

The troop leader radioed Evans, who was piloting the Skylark in a holding pattern at 10,000 feet in the Eastern Mediterranean. 'Captain Evans, we will be at the landing zone in approximately twenty minutes. I will contact you again before you land and confirm the area is secure for you to land.'

'Roger, roger,' was the reply from Evans as he started his planned entry into Lebanese airspace. He dropped the Skylark down to an altitude of 100 feet above sea level and silently approached his entry to landfall at a remote point between the towns of Halat and Ghazir. His airspeed of 300 mph enabled him to reach the Lebanese coast fifteen minutes after leaving his holding pattern. As the sea disappeared behind him, he constantly checked his radar screen for early warnings of any electric pylons, factory chimneys, or any other potential hazards unseen to him. Captain Evans also wore NV goggles, which would enable him to make out the hostage rescue party as he approached the landing zone.

Before they departed, Wilson went round the house and collected all mobile phones belonging to the kidnappers. He checked each device and saw that they were protected by fingerprint or facial recognition. His expertise would easily bypass these basic security systems, and the contents should provide an abundance of intelligence for the security services.

Sergeant McDonald groaned as he lifted the lifeless body of Tommy Roberts over his shoulder and led the party of troopers carrying Sven Solberg, with Mac taking up the rear with his Browning pistol in his free hand as he used all his strength to limp along, carrying the unconscious Kari Olsen in a fireman's lift. Thankfully for Mac, she was a light load compared to the wounded hostage and the dead weight of Trooper Roberts. He could see the others were struggling with their loads.

Unknown to Mac and the SAS team, the gunfire from the kidnapper which had killed Tommy Roberts had reverberated in the quiet forest and had awakened several families living further down the valley. The men immediately went into full alert, dressing quickly and grabbing weapons to defend their family and comrades as they had done so many times before. Calls were being made and a team of armed men were assembling to investigate the source of the gunfire.

As Mac and the SAS team approached the field designated as the landing zone, the drone operator confirmed that they were beginning to see activity further down the valley and a large group of men were gathering. The drone cameras were covering an area within a ten-mile radius of the landing zone.

At this point the American liaison officer Colonel John Jamieson intervened. He had become alarmed at the thought of a possible Hezbollah patrol getting involved in a firefight and the unthinkable loss of the Skylark helicopter. 'Men, we need to rapidly speed up this operation or I will abort. We have a window of approximately fifteen minutes before an enemy patrol will be entering the pick-up location.' The mention of the word *abort* sent shivers down the spines of Mac and the three remaining SAS soldiers.

The Skylark pilot had heard the statement from Colonel Jamieson as he approached the field. He increased his altitude to 1,000 feet and reduced the speed of the Skylark to 70 mph as he switched the two outer engines to the vertical position. This had the effect of almost bringing the aircraft to a stall before he switched the inner engines to the vertical position. The aircraft was now effectively a four-engined helicopter as the pilot skilfully brought the aircraft down into the middle of the field aided by a marker beacon set by McDonald. This manoeuvre had taken up seven of the fifteen minutes given by Colonel Jamieson.

With the turbofan engines of the Skylark still running, the only audible noise was the hum of the blades. McDonald raced forward and opened the cargo door, ready for loading to begin. As Mac approached the cargo door, Kari Olsen began to stir, giving out a low moan as fresh air began to clear the gas from her lungs. He lay her on the floor of the Skylark before climbing in and strapping the woman into the window seat. The SAS troopers carrying the unconscious body of Solberg were next as Mac and the sergeant helped slide the injured boy along the floor, trying to avoid jarring his injured leg. As the rest of the men crowded into the rear of the Skylark, Ross McDonald loaded the body of Trooper Roberts in and closed the rear door before scrambling into the co-pilot's seat and giving the Skylark pilot the thumbs up. Evans, hyper-aware of the deadline, increased the speed of the four engines and generated thrust as the aircraft overcame the weight of the load and began to lift off from the field just as Jamieson's fifteen-minute limit was reached.

The Hezbollah patrol had marched through the cedar forest towards the direction of the gunfire they suspected had come from a known Hezbollah safe house. The patrol leader set a fast pace and reached the edge of the clearing close to the house but saw nothing but darkness. The Hezbollah men could pick up a definite humming noise receding into the night sky, but nothing visible to the naked eye.

As the aircraft reached its optimum height, the pilot tilted all four engines to the horizontal position to enable him to fly the Skylark at top speed back to the USS *Lexington*, fully aware of the need to get the injured hostage hospital treatment as soon as possible. He flicked the radio to transmit.

'Skylark one to control. I am thirty-five minutes from base. Request emergency medical team for one injured party with gunshot wound to the upper leg.'

He received an instant 'Roger, roger. Will have medical team standing by.'

McDonald had been listening in on the co-pilot's headset and gave the Skylark pilot the thumbs up.

As the landing lights of the USS *Lexington* shone in the dark, the pilot slowed his speed down and dropped the Skylark to a suitable height before once again switching the position of the engines to vertical, allowing him to silently descend onto the deck of the aircraft carrier. The naval medical team began moving the barely conscious Sven Solberg onto a stretcher preparing to take him to the ship's medical centre.

A groggy Kari Olsen was still in a state of bewilderment, trying to fathom what she had gone through in the past few hours. She had fallen asleep as a hostage in captivity and woken up on board a silent helicopter, facing Rory McAdam and his fearsome looking, heavily armed troopers.

'Where am I and who are you?' Kari asked then gasped in horror as she saw for the first time a bloodied bandage on Sven's leg. Her hand went to her mouth, 'What happened to Sven? Is he badly injured?' Her questions were aimed at anyone who would answer her. Her shock went off the scale when she saw the bloodied body of the dead trooper lying on the floor of the helicopter.

Rory tried to reassure the woman. 'We're British Army and we have rescued you and Sven, with the help of our American friends.' As he turned and gestured towards the pilot. 'You are out of danger and in safe hands now. After some health checks and formalities, you will be able to return to Norway.' Mac pointed towards the injured man. 'Your friend will need some hospital treatment, but he will be in excellent hands here.' He lowered his voice as he looked at the body of Tommy Roberts.

'Unfortunately, in our business we take casualties.' Kari looked again at the dead man and felt nauseous and traumatised that a stranger had given his life to rescue her and Sven. A badly shaken Kari Olsen held on to Rory's arm for support as they left the helicopter and followed the troopers into the ship.

PART IV

Chapter Sixteen

Farah Halimi entered her boss's office and closed the door behind her. She noticed a copy of Cairo's daily newspaper lying on his desk. 'Please sit down, Farah.' He gestured to the chair across from him. 'Here in the embassy, we have a department that reads all the main newspapers from each European and Middle Eastern country to check any stories or developments of interest to us. Sometimes the foreign press and media provide information that we are not aware of and to confirm its accuracy we try and cross-check with other sources.'

Khaled Al Hussein paused to make sure she was focused. 'There is a headline in *Al Haram* which announced the brutal killing of a British oil worker employed by a Qatari company.' Al Hussein again paused to gauge any reaction from his words so far. Farah sat rigid and silent. She returned his gaze. 'Normally this may have been passed over as just another alcohol-fuelled fight that ended in tragedy. However, the story goes on to say that the only witness, a local taxi driver, saw the victim leave a club and was met by a woman outside the main gate. After a conversation the man accompanied the woman to her car and since then, there has been no further trace of the woman.'

Al Hussein looked across to Farah, who remained expressionless. He continued to the final part of his monologue. 'These facts would still not have aroused my interest, until I read the name of the victim – a forty-four-year-old Scottish man named William Flanagan. The same name that appears as your father on your birth certificate. I checked your recent vacation request and see that the estimated date for his death coincides with your visit to Cairo.'

Farah took a deep breath but held her composure in her reply, spoken softly but firmly. 'I took revenge on an inhuman savage who raped my mother and left her brutalised and pregnant. I have no regrets and am ready to accept the consequences.'

Al Hussein smiled at her response. 'My dear Farah, this man who destroyed your mother's life got what he deserved. Because you were smart enough to use false documents and cover your tracks, you are safe with us here in Paris. Only I know the connection between your birth certificate and this newspaper story.'

He let the words sink in before changing the subject. He brought out an enhanced photograph of a man taken in near darkness, with rain adding to the poor quality. 'This is a photograph of a man taken in the act of slaying a prince of Saudi Arabia, a murder which caused ramifications all the way to the top of our royal family.' Al Hussein passed the photograph over to Farah. 'We had a huge stroke of good fortune recently when a Palestinian doctor came to our embassy in Beirut and offered this information for sale. We paid him handsomely and we are now in the process of identifying this killer as a matter of urgency. This order has come from the very top of the royal family.'

Farah relaxed, knowing she was not about to be returned to Egypt and prison – or worse. 'How can I be of help? What can I do?' she asked cautiously.

Al Hussein opened a drawer in his desk and drew out another photograph of a man and passed it to Farah. This was a much clearer photo of a younger man dressed in a collar and tie, clean-shaven with a mop of fair hair. Farah studied the photograph as Al Hussein spoke. 'This is a photo of ex-army captain Andrew Fox, an asset we are developing in London. He has recently left the British Army and taken up a role in the Ministry of Defence. He's an asset who may provide high-class intelligence to us if handled properly. Discretion and patience will be the key for this project.'

Farah studied the photo for every little detail she could pick out: the colour of his eyes, the shape of his nose, his chin, his ears, and his complexion, just as her facial-recognition training had taught her.

'I want you to go to London and take over as his handler. He may be able to help us identify the assassin.'

Farah glanced at the other photo in front of her and then back at Andrew Fox's photo. 'Do we know anything else about him?'

Al Hussein leaned forward. 'He's mid-thirties, single, and desperate for money to maintain his way of life. He approached one of our embassy officials at a diplomatic cocktail party recently. We have already paid him £5,000 in cash as a sign of goodwill. Discreet enquiries found that although he comes from an upper-class background, he's broke, after losing everything in the recent stock market crash.'

Farah digested this information, studied the photograph again, and asked her boss, 'you said he was mid-thirties and single. He's quite handsome... so is he gay?'

Al Hussein gave her an engaging smile. 'That is for you to find out and exploit. You may even have to use a honey trap to get the outcome we need.'

After a further briefing on her unlimited budget, an apartment in Park Lane, and a new set of French identity documents, credit cards, and driving licence in the name of Julia Monet, Farah made her way to the embassy travel office to arrange a flight to London Heathrow and a new life under cover as a buyer of fine art for a rich Middle Eastern customer.

She had never considered the need to use a 'honey trap' and dreaded the thought of it but recognised that refusal of any part of this mission could mean a swift return to Cairo to face a murder charge. Her thoughts turned to Andrew Fox. *It could be worse – at least he is handsome and not too much older than me.* Anybody who saw her at that moment would have seen her eyes sparkle and a smile develop, accompanied by a skip in her step.

Chapter Seventeen

Captain Andrew Fox marched smartly into the major general's office on the command of 'Enter.' Fox stood before his commanding officer and snapped a perfect salute before taking the chair as ordered, in front of a vast oak table holding nothing except a telephone and a sheet of paper.

Andrew Fox was visibly nervous and slightly perplexed as to the reason for the meeting he had been ordered to attend. He had been in the parachute regiment for five years since graduating from Sandhurst Military Academy and held big ambitions to rise through the ranks just as his father and grandfather had done before him. His family were owners of a vast estate in Devon which included 160 acres of farmland, woodland, and moorland. He could trace the Fox family roots back to military service at Waterloo and the Peninsula Wars, supporting the Duke of Wellington.

The major general sat in silence, rereading the report in front of him and making sure he was armed with the facts before he began. 'Captain Fox.' He looked up to make sure he had his full attention. 'This is the action report of the incident of 12 September last year.' He paused to let the date register with Fox and continued. 'The ambush of the armoured reconnaissance patrol that you were commanding in Afghanistan.'

Andrew Fox gave a slight nod of the head and a growing

look of concern. He shuffled in his seat and awaited further information with some trepidation. 'Your patrol was halted in the Panjshir Valley by two explosive devices, IEDs as we know them, placed to immobilise the front and rear vehicles, resulting in the remaining vehicles being trapped in the narrow valley. Is this correct?'

'Yes, sir,' Fox replied without hesitation, growing fearful of where this was going.

The major general returned to the report. 'Your patrol came under sporadic fire from Taliban fighters hidden in the hillside and you took cover, hiding under an armoured car while your men awaited orders.' He looked into the eyes of Fox and repeated. 'You lay in the dirt under an armoured car instead of taking command of the situation, frozen into inaction by some gunfire. This is not the action we expect of an officer in the parachute regiment.'

Fox remained silent, looking down at the floor. With a visible shake of his head, the major general continued. 'It took two of your sergeants to find a solution to the mess you were in. They fixed the problem while you, the commanding officer, took cover, cowering underneath an armoured car. To compound this wretched behaviour, when you eventually made it back to your base in Musa Qala, you were overheard making disparaging remarks about your own commanding officer, who remained at the base and had been badly wounded rescuing a pilot from a burning helicopter – an action above and beyond the call of duty, for which he was rightly awarded the Victoria Cross and the American Medal of Honour.'

The major general fixed a stare on Andrew Fox. 'You were heard to call Major McAdam...' He paused. 'A fucking glory hunter!'

Andrew Fox bowed his head in a mixture of shame and guilt. He knew he had spoken out of turn back then but had hoped it would blow over with the passage of time. The major general wanted to conclude this distasteful dressing-down now that it was clear that Captain Fox had nothing to say in reply.

'You have two choices, Captain Fox: a written apology to Major McAdam or a written resignation of your commission. The choice is yours.'

As he left the room, Fox could barely hide his anger and contempt at the outcome of the action report and the options offered by his commanding officer. He knew that this black mark on his record would halt any advancement in the army even if he furnished a letter of apology to Rory McAdam. That evening, he wrote his letter of resignation, abandoning a career which had promised so much but had come to a premature end.

Chapter Eighteen

Andrew Fox was at a loss. His life back in London was very different from the institutional organisation of army life. Even over the phone his mother could hear signs of desperation in his voice as he began to lose hope of finding a suitable job that could fund his lifestyle. Finally, his mother made a call to her brother, Giles Rankin, who held the position of operations director and beseeched him to use his reputation and status to find her son a position within the Ministry of Defence.

Giles Rankin held great influence within the MOD and when he recommended the name of Andrew Fox for the position of liaison officer, nobody questioned the endorsement or conducted any background checks. Fox started his work at a lower salary than his previous employment but was grateful for the opportunity his uncle Giles had given him. As a liaison officer his role involved many interdepartmental meetings between MOD staff and senior officers of the Royal Air Force, who were supplying training personnel and equipment to the Royal Saudi Air Force in support of a multi-billion-pound contract between BAE and the government of Saudi Arabia to supply the latest generation Tornado fighter aircraft.

After one particularly tough day negotiating with the Saudi Air Force representatives, Fox had been surprised to be invited to a social event organised by the Saudi embassy military attaché. 'Just a quiet drink at a Turkish Bar and Grill to seal our deal,' was the request which a surprised Andrew Fox readily accepted.

The quiet drink included a sumptuous meal of grilled lamb and chicken accompanied by several bottles of wine, on top of the several large gins already consumed. With his tongue well and truly loosened, Andrew Fox began to open up about his personal life. 'I love the company of women, but I'm an extremely shy man, believe it or not. The more attractive the girl is, the greater my lack of confidence.' Fox paused to let this sink in to the two Saudi men sharing his table. After some casual banter back and forth on the subject of women, the military attaché waited until his colleague excused himself, leaving him alone at the table with a tipsy Andrew Fox.

'There's a girl who works for a friend of mine. A beautiful French girl who is single and would be a perfect match for you.' He continued, 'She lives here in London and has very few friends outside her work. Would you like me to arrange for you to meet her?'

He had definitely got Fox's attention, and Fox could barely hide his eagerness. 'Yes, I would love to meet her. A French woman sounds much more appealing than the few dreary English girls I know.'

When his colleague returned to the table, the attaché stood up to signal the end of the evening. As they shook hands and said their farewells and thanks, the attaché quietly leaned forward with a smile and said, 'Leave it with me. I'll be in touch soon.'

* * *

Farah had been given time off by the embassy to settle into her new life and home in London. The penthouse apartment in London's West End, with stunning views over Hyde Park, was ideally situated to allow Farah to walk around central London, get her bearings, and familiarise herself with her surroundings. Shopping was easy with an unlimited budget and Farah purchased a variety of outfits, both elegant and casual, always remembering to sign the credit card slips in the name of Juliet Monet. Her mini vacation ended when she received a call from her new boss, the Mabahith man at the London embassy.

Although the Saudi embassy in Mayfair was close to her apartment, the meeting took place on a remote park bench overlooking the Serpentine Lake in Hyde Park. After his introduction, Jamal Nasir, the man who would be her controller in London, went on to brief Farah on the new source they were developing at the British Ministry of Defence.

'Andrew Fox is a complex young man with expensive tastes but without the money to finance them. We will help him fund his lifestyle in return for a little information.' He looked into Farah's eyes. 'You will be my contact to facilitate payments and receive low-key intelligence.'

Farah smiled with a little trepidation before asking, 'Will payments be in the form of cash or in kind?'

Jamal Nasir smiled before replying. 'My dear Farah, you will have to manage the situation as it develops, but it may be a combination of both.'

He paused then added, 'With your training and experience, you will be more than able to cope with whatever life throws at you. If handled properly, Andrew Fox will be like a puppy in your capable hands.'

RETRIBUTION

* * *

Andrew Fox had completed another round of talks with his Saudi embassy customers, who never missed a chance to remind him of the value of the contracts they were finalising, the importance of these contracts to British manufacturing, and the jobs and revenue they produced. At the end of the day's negotiations, the Saudi military attaché took Andrew Fox aside and asked him if he was still interested in a date with the French woman he had previously mentioned.

'Yes, one hundred per cent,' was his enthusiastic answer. It had been two weeks since Fox had last been out on a date and that had turned out to be a tedious night with a dull woman from the MOD office, who he had managed to avoid meeting again despite several missed calls and ignored messages on his mobile phone.

* * *

As Farah left her apartment and walked to the waiting car, the figure-hugging black and silver dress emphasised her slim athletic figure and was finished off with a discreet diamond necklace and matching bracelet. The chauffeur couldn't resist a low whistle to himself as she climbed into the back seat of the car. The driver headed for a French restaurant tucked away in the corner of Westbourne Grove in a quiet area of Notting Hill. As the maître d' showed her to the table, Andrew Fox rose to his feet, almost speechless at the stunning woman in front of him. She gave him a sparkling smile and held out her hand. 'Hi, I'm Juliet.'

Fox took her hand and replied, 'Bonsoir, mademoiselle Juliet. The pleasure is all mine.' He bent and kissed the back of her hand, hoping to make an instant impression. She laughed at the old-fashioned greeting, happy inside that he was making the effort.

As the evening progressed, it became clear that they were hitting it off. A meal of scallops and roast fennel was washed down with an excellent Sancerre and the chatter was almost non-stop. A good sign, she thought, as there were no awkward moments or any prolonged gaps in conversation. They were the last couple to leave the restaurant, and Andrew Fox was flabbergasted when he requested the bill, only to be told it had already been taken care of in advance.

'I take it our mutual friend was behind this,' whispered a happy and somewhat relieved Fox as he opened the door of the taxi. Farah contemplated her options. She had time on her side and wanted to make him wait until she was ready, and he was nearing desperation.

As the taxi stopped outside her apartment, she leaned over and kissed him on the cheek, giving him a sensuous waft of her expensive perfume. 'Thank you for a wonderful evening. I hope we can meet again.'

A somewhat crestfallen Andrew Fox hid his disappointment that the evening was clearly over. 'Thank you for a fabulous evening. I really enjoyed it.'

Farah opened her clutch bag and pulled out her business card. 'Call me,' she said as she handed him the card and left the taxi without looking back.

She knew that she now had him eating out of the palm of her hand. Farah was no stranger to men and had had several casual relationships while at university.

Several dates later, with the farewell kiss on the cheek now moving to a lingering kiss on the lips, Farah decided to move the relationship up to the next level. He couldn't hide his delight at the call she made one Thursday evening. 'I'm going to Paris for the weekend. Would you like to join me?'

Almost as she finished the question, Fox answered her. 'Yes, that would be wonderful. I've been there a few times before, but never really got to know Paris. I can't wait.' *Paris*, he thought, *with a beautiful woman and a whole weekend to spend together.* Things were finally beginning to look up in the life of Andrew Fox.

* * *

When Farah and Andrew arrived, her familiarity of Paris and the Parisian way of life soon became clear. 'We will take the metro into the city,' she announced as they cleared immigration and collected their bags. 'Everyone takes the metro here. It's cheap, quick, and efficient, unlike the taxi service.' She laughed as they joined the crowds heading for central Paris.

After changing trains at Les Halles, they got off at Concorde metro station and walked holding hands to the Hotel de Carillon. As they checked in, Fox found that all charges had been taken care of ahead of time. 'It's okay,' she reassured him. 'This is a working weekend for me, so it's covered by business expenses. Besides, my client is one of the wealthiest men in the Middle East. I choose works of art for him to buy and he pays me an excellent salary and all my expenses.'

After they dropped off their bags, she took his hand and led him out. 'Come on, let me show you the real Paris.'

They spent the rest of the morning exploring the Latin Quarter with its narrow cobblestone streets and ancient buildings which had been spared during the redevelopment of

Paris. Farah pointed out the Sorbonne where she had attended university, the Pantheon shrine paying tribute to the heroes of French history, and the Lutèce arena which dated back to Roman times. They made their way to the food market on Rue Mouffetard where they enjoyed a lunch of French cheeses and wine. Then they took the metro to the Bohemian district of Montmartre, where they walked around, taking in the arts and crafts of the hilltop district before returning, exhausted, to their hotel room.

While Farah excused herself to go to the bathroom, Fox took a small confidence-building pill from his pocket, slipped it into his mouth, and washed it down with a glass of water. When Farah returned from the bathroom, she wore a bathrobe covering her black lace underwear. She approached him, trying to be casual and relaxed, seeing he was clearly nervous. She put her arms around his neck and pulled him towards her before engaging in a long, passionate kiss. After more kissing, he untied her robe and slipped it off her shoulders, kissing her exposed neck and chest. She gave a lustful sigh as he unfastened her bra and continued kissing her all over her chest and nipples.

He took her hand and led a smiling Farah to lie on top of the bed where more kissing was followed by sexual intercourse with a tender and mutual satisfaction. The pill that Andrew Fox had taken was working to perfection and twice more they made love that evening before showering, dressing, and taking a late supper in the hotel restaurant. Their relationship now sealed, Fox began to relax and enjoy this precious time with his new partner. Farah also relaxed but for different reasons. She had achieved the first part of her mission and now exerted a degree of control and influence over a British Ministry of Defence employee. The remainder of the weekend flew by with frequent copulation in between visits to the Louvre and walks around the Petite Ceinture, the little-known old railway line that ran around Paris.

Andrew Fox asked many questions about her earlier life in Paris, and she was able to answer most of them truthfully and some with a plausible lie. She did not go into details about her parents other than to say they had both died when she was a teenager. Her sadness at the subject dissuaded any further questions from Fox. He was equally coy when she asked him about his army career, and he was happy to change the subject to avoid any more awkward questions.

* * *

They decided on their flight back to Heathrow that Andrew would take the Heathrow Express to Paddington, where he had a five-minute walk to his house. Farah would take the underground train to Hyde Park Corner where she had a ten-minute walk to her apartment. Although Fox was like a lovesick puppy at their parting, Farah had a slight sense of relief to be alone again and reminded herself of the mission she had accepted and the sacrifice she'd had to make with her body, but she deliberately guarded her heart and soul from any thoughts of romance.

As she exited the underground station, she scanned the view ahead of her and noticed a scruffy guy at the top of the steps, checking the handful of passengers that passed him. She glanced out of the corner of her eye as she passed him and saw him smile, accompanied by a definite glint in his eye. Her training and natural instincts told her that she had caught his attention, and he began following her, keeping the distance behind her to around thirty metres. Farah was now on full alert as she began to take the anti-surveillance steps she had been taught. She varied the pace of her walking, speeding up, and then slowing down, and using the mirrors of parked cars to check her pursuer's positioning.

She paused to look into the shop window of a car showroom packed with sports cars and luxury SUVs. As she glanced backwards, she saw the man pause and pretend to look into a shop window, and in that moment, Farah had her confirmation as the man stood looking into a shop selling upmarket baby clothes and accessories. She continued walking in the early evening light, completely familiar with her route home and aware that the man following her was now rapidly closing the gap between them.

Farah was experiencing an adrenalin spike, hypervigilant to the threat, believing her life may be in mortal danger. To confirm that he was following her with no good intentions, she turned into a lane that ran alongside an office block a few minutes from the front door of her apartment block. The lane she had deliberately chosen was a dead end and unlit. She walked halfway down with her senses fully alert.

She stopped and turned to face the man who was almost skipping towards her now as he closed in on his victim, reaching under his navy-blue hoodie to pull out a short knife with a vicious-looking serrated top edge. 'Okay, rich bitch, give me your money and mobile phone,' he snarled. 'Hurry up or I'll cut your pretty face, bitch.' Farah stood facing him square on, her legs spread apart and her knees slightly bent, perfectly balanced as she pushed her weekend bag to the side of the road and kept her eyes firmly on her attacker.

She decided to give him a warning first but already knew it would be a waste of her breath. 'Please, don't do this. Walk away while you still can.' Her determined look and warning message, delivered a few octaves lower than her normal speech, had the opposite effect as he laughed at her and raised his right arm which held the knife, ready to strike. As he took a step closer to Farah, closing the gap enough so she could smell the alcohol on his breath and see his drug-enlarged pupils, she knew the situation had reached the point of no return.

Farah made a chewing motion with her mouth, producing a pool of saliva, tilted her head back slightly, and, as forcibly as she could, spat the liquid straight at his eyes, resulting in her attacker crying out in a mixture of shock and surprise, which caught him momentarily off guard. He put his free hand up to his face, trying to clear his eyes, as his vision was obscured. In one swift movement, Farah executed a combination of movements as she reached up and took a firm grip of the wrist holding the knife and swung her right leg in a savage kick to his groin, causing him to scream in pain as both legs gave way and he collapsed to the ground.

As he fell, Farah twisted his wrist with a fierce half-turn until the knife dropped to the ground with a metallic clatter. Still holding on to his wrist, she held his arm to the ground before stamping hard on his exposed arm. She heard a satisfying crack as she snapped his wrist bone. The man's groan was muffled by the stream of yellow vomit from his mouth. He was barely conscious with extreme pain in his groin and a broken wrist. Farah was now in full attack mode and stood over his prone body. Moving to his left leg, she stamped on the bone just above his ankle and was rewarded by another audible crack.

She stood back to survey her would-be attacker and noted the knife lying by his unconscious body. She calmly picked up the knife and leaned close to his head, whispering, 'A kiss from the rich bitch,' then she cut an X on each cheek, deep enough to scar him for life, but not deep enough to cause him to bleed to death.

She collected her weekend bag and headed back to the main street where she wiped the handle clean before dropping the knife in a waste bin and heading to her apartment to relax and lower her adrenalin levels back to normal.

The Metropolitan Police incident report noted the location and estimated time of the attack on Sylvester Harrison, a well-known criminal with an extensive record for violence and robbery. The victim had been heard calling out for help from a darkened alleyway around two hours after the initial attack. The passer-by had called the police and an ambulance and walked on, satisfied that he had done his duty as a good citizen but reluctant to get involved any further.

The two police officers followed the ambulance back to the Accident & Emergency department of St Thomas's Hospital, where the victim received twenty-four stitches to the cuts on both cheeks. The fractures to his ankle and forearm required pins to be inserted to allow the bones to knit together, and both limbs were encased in heavy plaster of Paris. The damaged fingers were bandaged together, and time alone would eventually heal them.

When questioned by the police officers, Harrison refused to give any answers. The only reaction noted was an ironic smile when the senior officer asked, 'Do you know the identity of the man who inflicted such serious injuries on you?'

Since it was clear that no information was forthcoming and there were no witnesses, the understaffed and under-resourced police filed the report as 'inconclusive' and moved on to their next case.

Chapter Nineteen

After their romantic weekend in Paris, Andrew Fox bombarded his newfound girlfriend with a blizzard of messages to her mobile phone, asking when they could next meet up. Clearly the lovestruck man was presuming mutual feelings, but although she had hated using her body to trap the unsuspecting man, Farah had a bigger objective in mind.

On her return to London, she had met up again with her boss from the Saudi Arabian embassy and brought him up to date. 'The first part of my mission has been successful, and I can confirm Andrew Fox is not gay. I now have him in a position where I can ask for his help in identifying this killer,' she said, pointing to the photograph of Rory McAdam, adding, 'Assuming, of course, that he is British, as your experts in Riyadh think.'

Her boss Jamal Nasir could not contain his joy at the progress she had made. 'My dear Farah, we appreciate that you have had to sacrifice yourself in this cause and it must have been most unpleasant having to build a false relationship with this kaffir. I can assure you that you will be very well rewarded for your efforts, no matter how distasteful this has been for you. As you know, we need a name, and then we need to find this man and terminate him at the earliest opportunity.' Nasir added, 'We have sources in America and France who have run the photograph through a facial-recognition program, but both have failed to put a name to the face.' He paused, then said, 'We are convinced that the assassin is either working for British intelligence or for Mossad.'

Farah finally answered one of Fox's many messages asking to meet up with her again. Over drinks at one of London's classy French wine bars, she explained that she had been in meetings with her client, choosing which works of art she was to track down and try to purchase on his behalf. Money would be no object for the right piece of art.

'How much is your budget?' an inquisitive Andrew Fox asked.

Farah answered him with a laugh. 'Enough to buy anything that's up for sale. Do you have anything you want to offload?' Fox shook his head, a little intimidated by her spending power. As they finished their third glass of wine, she decided to make her move. She looked him straight in the eyes and gave him a sensuous smile.

'Can we go back to your place tonight? I have something to show you.'

Fox was smitten with the woman before him and stammered his reply. 'Absolutely, my place is only ten or fifteen minutes from here by taxi.'

After an hour of passionate lovemaking where she took the initiative, she lay in his arms and took the opportunity to bring up the subject of a face in a photograph that her boss in Abu Dhabi was trying to identify. Would he be good enough to run it through a facial-recognition program at his office and see if it could put a name to the face?

Fox readily agreed with the comment, 'I don't see what harm it could do. What does he want the man's name for?'

She delayed her answer before giving him a shrug of her shoulders. 'It's something about an unpaid debt, but I don't have the details,' she said before kissing him on his neck and shoulders as she worked her way down his body.

* * *

Over coffee the next morning, before he left for the office, she pulled out the enhanced A4-sized photograph given to her by Jamal Nasir. 'This is the guy my boss is trying to find a name for,' she said as she passed it to Fox.

He looked at the image for a few seconds before replying in a low voice. 'I don't need to run this through a computer. I know exactly who this is.' He shook his head, his voice going up a few octaves. 'My God, it's a small world. This Scottish bastard Rory McAdam helped finish my career in the army. And now he's in debt! I will gladly help anyone against him.'

Farah could not believe what she was hearing and encouraged him to give her more. 'If you know his name, can you find out where he lives?'

Fox was barely able to contain his enthusiasm as he leaned over the table to kiss her. 'My darling, for you, anything. Give me a few days and I will not only have his address, but also his shoe size and inside-leg measurements.' He laughed at his own joke, totally ignorant of the true purpose of her request.

Chapter Twenty

Enjoying a mid-morning coffee as his wife hovered over the twins, who were blissfully asleep after their morning feed, Mac's tranquillity was broken by the dogs barking. He looked up as he heard the video doorbell alarm at the front gate go off. Picking up his mobile phone, he saw a young man who did not have the appearance of a regular hiker. Speaking to the visitor through his phone, he asked the smartly dressed young man, 'How can I help you?'

The man looked into the camera device on the doorbell and cleared his throat. 'I'm Jamie Wylde, a reporter from the *Press and Journal*. I'd like to ask you a few questions on the shooting incident earlier this year, which resulted in a helicopter rescue and a lot of army activity in the area afterwards.'

Both Mac and his wife had dreaded the time when they would have to face something like this. In such a quiet and isolated area, it was impossible to expect an attempted murder to go unreported. Such a major shooting incident at their cottage on the edge of the Balmoral estate would inevitably attract media attention.

Mac pleaded ignorance and stuck to the story that he and his wife had both been out of the country at the time and couldn't help with any information. The reporter became very insistent, challenging Mac that he must know something about the incident. And who had been staying at the cottage if they, as the owners, had not been there?

He persisted. 'You must know who was staying in your house if, as you say, you were abroad. Did you rent the house out or let friends or family stay?' Mac was getting exasperated hearing this relentless questioning and gave up the discussion over video.

He opened the door and spoke forcibly to the reporter. 'It's none of your bloody business who stays in our house. I will give you ten seconds to get your arse away from my front gate.'

The reporter was experienced enough to know there would be trouble if he continued his line of questioning. 'Okay, I'll just have to check with other sources. Have a nice day.' With that, Jamie Wylde turned and began his long trek back to the car park.

After a long telephone discussion with his boss in Century House in London, Mac sat down with his wife, ready for a difficult conversation, knowing how much his wife loved the place. 'Jaz, we need to move. If a reporter from a local newspaper can track us down, then we might as well stick a sign on the roof saying *The McAdam family live here.*' Jaz gave an audible sigh as she nodded in agreement.

'I knew after I was discharged from hospital that we'd need to move. It's not safe here. Anyway, we'll need some place closer to nurseries and schools as the twins grow up. We can't be driving thirty miles a day to take the children back and forth to Ballater. Imagine the travelling in the winter.' Mac agreed, hiding his surprise at how easy a conversation this had been. Later that evening Mac was busy on the internet, looking at the houses available in or around his home city of Aberdeen.

* * *

The editor of the *Press and Journal* sat across the table listening to the local police commander, as Susan Den read out the text of the paper she held in her hand. The editor's astonishment grew by the second as he realised what the police commander was reading out before asking him to sign two copies of the document, one which she kept, and the other was passed to the shocked editor.

'This is actually a *D-Notice?*' he asked, still trying to comprehend the incredible news. 'The *Press and Journal* have never been served a D-Notice since we first started publishing in 1747. What in the name of God has Jamie Wylde done to deserve this?'

Susan Den shrugged her shoulders and smiled back at the man. 'I'm only the messenger, Jim. The notice originated from a government committee that's responsible for national security pertaining to public information.' With that, Susan Den rose from her chair, shook the editor's hand, and left the room knowing she had served her first and probably last ever government notice preventing a publication on the grounds of national security.

* * *

Mac and Jaz took the momentous step of giving up the cottage on the shores of Loch Muick and moving back to Aberdeen. As the last of the boxes were loaded into the removal van, Mac turned to his wife. 'Don't worry, Jaz. We still have it for weekends and school holidays. The house will stay in the family just as my grandfather wished when it was gifted to me.'

The move to River Don Lodge was easier than both had imagined. Situated in land that followed the bend on the river

Don, it was directly across the river from the popular Seaton Park. Jaz couldn't hide her delight. 'Oh, Mac, it's beautiful and we have the best of both worlds. We're in the country but ten minutes from the nursery and fifteen minutes from the shops. I love it and I know the twins will grow to love it too. So much fresh air and greenery right on our doorstep.'

Chapter Twenty-One

Andrew Fox knew that Rory McAdam had left the army on a medical discharge but did not know where he'd gone thereafter. His call to the Army Records Department at the Ministry of Defence was met with a blank reply that stated *No known career upon discharge*. His request triggered an alert inside the administration of the MOD that ultimately landed on the desk of his uncle, the operations director.

Giles Rankin did not beat about the bush with his nephew and asked sternly, 'Why are you asking for details on an ex-soldier by the name of Rory McAdam?'

Fox was taken aback that his casual enquiry had made its way all the way up to the operations director. 'I was only asking so that I could meet up with Rory for a beer. He was my commanding officer in Afghanistan and I'm heading up to Scotland soon, so it would be good to see him again. I'm surprised by the reaction. I only asked if they had an address for him.'

His uncle gave an understanding smile. 'Andrew, Rory McAdam is engaged in some very sensitive government business, so it's natural for alarm bells to ring when someone enquires about his whereabouts. It's good that the people in the Army Records Office are on the ball and did their job correctly. I'll get this matter closed so we can get on with our work. We're both busy men.' Fox visibly relaxed and started to head for the door as his uncle casually added, 'He's back in Aberdeen at a new house he and his wife have bought. River Don Lodge, but that stays between me and you.'

* * *

Farah knew of the city of Aberdeen but had never heard of Seaton Park or River Don Lodge. In less than two minutes on Google Maps, she had a location and an address. Jamal Nasir, the head of Mabahith in the Saudi embassy in London, could barely contain himself when Farah brought news of the killer in the photograph. Not only did she have a name, but also a home address of an isolated lodge, remote from any neighbours or members of the public. Nasir ordered a Saudi royal family private jet to take him from London to Riyadh. This kind of news needed to be delivered in person if his career was to benefit from this sensational breakthrough.

The Saudi private jet took off from Oxford and less than six hours later, Nasir was seated before the Saudi head of Mabahith and three royal princes who were closely related to the Beirut murder victim Ahmed Salah bin Saud. Pointing to the photograph, he addressed the men respectfully. 'The assassin is Rory McAdam, a Scottish man who was once an officer in the British Army. He murdered our dear brother Ahmed in cold blood.' There were gasps of surprise before Jamal Nasir continued. 'We also know the address of his house in Scotland and its location is ideal for a revenge strike. Although it's in a city, it's in an isolated location with a large piece of uninhabited land around the house.'

The gasps of surprise had now turned into exclamations of appreciation. 'How did you manage to get this priceless information?'

Jamal Nasir knew he would have to share the credit. 'We set a honey trap with our female field agent, who managed to penetrate an asset at the British Ministry of Defence, and he identified the killer and gave her his home address.'

The astonishment was clear to see and hear from the four Saudis in the room. 'You have a woman capable of this? Who is she?' asked the most senior of the royal princes present.

Jamal Nasir turned to the head of Mabahith and said, 'You remember the French-born Algerian girl, Farah Halimi?' His boss nodded. 'She has turned into my most valuable agent in the field. She alone is responsible for obtaining the information. I simply arranged for her to meet with the man from the British Ministry of Defence, but the rest of the work was down to her and her alone.'

The tension in the room was high as Jamal Nasir outlined the scheme to terminate the killer and exact the necessary revenge. 'She will travel to Aberdeen and carry out surveillance on McAdam then come back to me with a plan to complete this mission, while leaving no trace for the British police. She will work alone to remain above suspicion and there will be no mobile phone or computer contact. The British security agencies have a very good record of intelligence tracking as you know, so only face-to-face communications will be allowed.'

His boss nodded his head in agreement and informed him, 'There will be no timescale on this operation. We don't want any mistakes because we rushed. You can tell Farah Halimi her bonus upon completion of this task will be beyond the dreams of any woman.' He also reminded Jamal Nasir of the need for the operation to be completely untraceable back to Saudi Arabia.

Chapter Twenty-Two

After flying into Aberdeen's Dyce airport, Farah rented a white BMW car and drove to a rented apartment in the north of the city, around two miles from Seaton Park and the River Don Lodge. All travel, accommodation, and car rental were booked under the name of Julia Monet, a French-born woman now resident in London. Her first walk through the busy park gave her a chance to get her bearings. The park was bordered by the river Don on one side and the busy King Street on the other. The western side of the park was dominated by the huge cathedral of St Machar and its ancient graveyard.

McAdam's property was on the far side of the river and stood alone. Farah had looked up the history of the building and found that it had once been a hunting lodge dating back to the fourteenth century. Now modernised and extended with a long sloping driveway connecting it to the shared driveway of the house that was once the home of Thomas Blake Glover, the Scottish founder of Japan's Mitsubishi Corporation. As she walked along the riverbank, looking across to the lodge, Farah turned her eyes to the left. At the top of the hill, running parallel with the river, her attention was drawn to a block of apartments with the upper floors giving an excellent all-round view of Seaton Park, with the lodge directly across the river.

She knew immediately where she wanted her accommodation for the duration of this mission to be. There would be no better location to observe the activity within the grounds of the lodge discreetly. Her next task would be to try and lease or buy an upper-floor apartment. She immediately started work on this by contacting the property centre in Aberdeen to see if any apartments in this block were up for sale or lease, only to be told that none of the properties at this address were available. She made an appointment to meet with Robert Taylor, the property manager at one of Aberdeen's biggest estate agents.

'I've recently separated from my husband and received a substantial settlement,' was how she opened the meeting with him. 'I have fallen in love with the apartments in Gordon's Mills Road, and their beautiful views over the river and the park. I will pay well above market price to rent or buy an upper-floor apartment.'

Taylor had heard many strange requests before regarding properties, but someone willing to throw big money on a property close to the Tillydrone housing estate was a first for him. Robert Taylor considered her request and her determination to obtain a property and typed the address into his computer. 'Since the database shows there is nothing currently on the market for sale or rent, I suggest we contact the current tenants of these apartments with an offer of a lease attractive enough for them to consider renting out their property.'

Without hesitation, Farah agreed to this proposal, which set Taylor typing into the database. After several minutes, he found a similar rental agreement for an apartment from a few years earlier. He turned the screen of his computer round to show Farah the layout of the accommodation and explained that 'This apartment is on the first floor and was leased by a university lecturer from nearby Aberdeen University for £600 per month.'

Farah paid no attention to the details of the apartment and replied, 'I will pay £3,000 per month for a furnished top-floor apartment. As an extra incentive I will also offer to pay the rent for the people vacating their property.'

Taylor furrowed his brow as he picked up on her apparent reckless desperation. 'I can find you other properties with great river views in a more desirable area for that kind of budget. Deeside, for instance, has some fantastic houses available now on our property register with immediate entry.'

Farah shook her head. 'Thank you but no. This is the only property location for me.'

Taylor got the message. 'I'll get my assistant straight onto the case. I have your mobile number and will call you when we have anything suitable.'

Robert Taylor smiled as he shook her hand. 'Madam Monet, we will do our best as we always do for our clients.'

After an hour of knocking on doors on the upper floors of the six apartment blocks, it was the door of single mum Jody Miller where Robert Taylor's enthusiastic assistant met with success. 'You mean this client of yours will pay me £3,000 per month in rent and pay for my rent somewhere else? Are you sure that's what she's offering?'

Georgia Hewitt, Taylor's assistant, smiled back at the astonished look on Jody's face. 'Yes, I double-checked this with my boss before heading out here. Reading between the lines, I think if you wanted to push it, you could get your utility bills covered at your new property too. She appears to be pretty desperate and flush with cash too.'

Jody invited the young woman into the top-floor apartment and told her she was free to look around while she made some tea. Trying to contain her excitement, Jody phoned her father and told him of the offer. As expected, Jody's father agreed the offer was too good to refuse. 'It's a no-brainer, Jody. Three grand a month and she's paying the rent for another place for you and wee Leon... go for it, girl, before she changes her mind or finds somewhere else.'

'Me and my dad both think it's a great offer, but I don't want the upheaval of moving for anything less than at least a one-year lease.'

Georgia Hewitt pulled out her mobile phone and confirmed to her boss she had found a suitable apartment. 'Does it have a commanding view over the river and the park, Georgia?' he asked.

She walked over to the living-room window. 'Absolutely. Perfect views over the Don Valley and all the way into Seaton Park. That was the precondition, wasn't it? This ticks all the boxes.' Georgia turned and smiled at Jody as she continued, 'Robert, the tenant has a couple of small stipulations.'

Robert Taylor made an audible groan. 'Okay, what are they?'

'A minimum one-year lease period and all utilities and taxes at the other rental property to be paid by our client.'

Taylor cheered up at the news. 'I'm sure this will be acceptable. Tell the tenant that I will visit her with my client tomorrow morning at ten thirty.'

As Taylor suspected, a delighted Farah Halimi readily accepted the additional costs. At ten thirty the next day, Farah met Robert Taylor in the car park of River View Court before they took the elevator to the top floor to meet Jody Miller. The apartment had always been kept in good condition, but since the news of the rental client coming the next morning, Jody had been busy giving the home an extra wash and polish and tidying up her young son's bedroom.

After Taylor had introduced Farah as Julia Monet, he left Jody to show her round the house, pointing out the extra cupboards she had installed, the power shower in the bathroom, and the modern smart TV equipment and ultra-fast Wi-Fi. While it was definitely not Mayfair, Farah showed a grateful interest in all that Jody showed her, with her total focus on the view into River Don Lodge. She was not disappointed – the lodge was in full view, sparkling in the summer sunshine.

'It's perfect. How soon can I move in?' Farah asked, barely able to control her enthusiasm.

That afternoon, Jody Miller started looking through the properties available for rent in and around Aberdeen. She narrowed the search down to the area close by as she wanted to keep her son in the same school. She quickly found a vacant property a ten-minute walk away from where she already lived. Don Street was a pleasant street in a quiet area of Tillydrone and still within easy walking distance for her son's school. When she arranged to visit the property that evening, Jody Miller was delighted. The house was part furnished, clean, and ready for immediate entry.

* * *

Jody used Robert Taylor to arrange the new lease documents, and she organised a standing order for the gas, electric, and council-tax bills that Julia Monet had generously agreed to pay. After she signed the lease document to hand over her house to Julia Monet, Jody's curiosity got the better of her.

'Mr Taylor, I have a nice house with nice views. It's not the most desirable area in the city, but it's not the worst either. Why would someone with her budget be so keen to live on Gordon's Mills Road?'

Taylor laughed as he began to answer her question. 'Please, don't take this the wrong way, and I don't mean to cause offence, but Georgia and I have been asking the same question since Julia Monet came into our office and specified Gordon's Mills Road, and no other alternatives. It's baffling us too, but she's paid our invoice, and you will have a minimum of £36,000 in rental income, plus living virtually cost-free for the next twelve months.'

Jody shrugged and smiled. 'I'm moving out on Friday morning and will drop off the keys to your office on Friday afternoon. Is that okay?'

Robert rose and shook Jody's hand. 'Perfect, Jody. It was a pleasure doing business with you. Keep in touch and the best of luck to you and young Leon.'

Chapter Twenty-Three

Farah settled into her new accommodation and made an online purchase of a pair of high-power binoculars complete with a tripod support stand. The panorama from the living-room window gave Farah a perfect view into River Don Lodge where she watched the comings and goings of a woman, she presumed to be Rory McAdam's wife or partner. After two weeks of surveillance, Farah had worked out a pattern of the woman driving two kids to nursery school each morning, Monday to Friday, in her Toyota hatchback. On returning from the school run, she would park her car next to Rory McAdam's pick-up truck. Weekends saw the kids playing in the garden, walking in the park, and occasionally eating meals at the patio table when the sun came out. Since moving into the apartment, Farah had seen no sign of her target, Rory McAdam, and the pick-up truck hadn't moved once.

It was a month after moving into the apartment that Farah's patience finally paid off. One evening as she sat at the window sipping a glass of white wine, her attention was alerted by a pair of headlights coming down the driveway approaching the lodge. The lights belonged to a taxi which had drawn up outside the front door. After a short delay, the passenger door opened and out stepped Rory McAdam with a holdall, to be met at the door by his wife, who greeted him with a passionate kiss and a prolonged embrace. Farah's hand tightened round her binoculars as her pulse quickened and the hint of a smile grew. Four long weeks of observing and noting down all comings and goings from the house had finally been rewarded.

Another ten days of surveillance by Farah confirmed that the arrival of McAdam had not changed the woman's early morning and mid-afternoon school runs. After following him at a discreet distance, Farah knew that Rory McAdam would leave the house and drive his pick-up truck three times a week to visit a physiotherapist. Farah assumed this was for treatment to a damaged leg, which was causing him to walk with a distinct limp. Every Monday, Wednesday, and Friday, Rory McAdam would leave the house at the same time and return around the same time. She noted down the time on every occasion she saw McAdam, or his wife drive away from the house and return.

Farah did the long drive from Aberdeen to London for a face-to-face meeting with her Saudi boss at the same bench as their previous meeting in leafy Hyde Park. 'I've established a pattern in his lifestyle which should present me with an opportunity for an isolated hit on Rory McAdam with no danger to anyone else.' Her boss showed no emotion as he gestured for her to continue. 'I'm planning to take him out in his own vehicle while it's still in his driveway. His wife and family do the morning school run before he leaves the house for a regular visit to his physio.'

Her boss broke into a smile. 'I like the idea of an isolated hit with no danger to anyone else. Our retribution is for the assassin Rory McAdam and no one else.'

Farah relaxed a little at his sign of acceptance. 'I will need a detonator and an electronic trigger device, the same as I used in my training with the Algerians. In fact, I will need two of them to cover all eventualities. The rest of the material I will buy locally to manufacture my weapon.'

With the tacit agreement of her boss, she did the long return drive to Aberdeen carrying the detonator and two small electronic trigger devices which resembled an electronic stopwatch. She quickly resumed her observation of the lifestyle patterns of McAdam and his wife. With no changes obvious, Farah began assembling the materials she would need using items purchased with cash from regular everyday shops around Aberdeen.

During her training with the Algerians, Farah had been taught how to handle, mix and prepare a range of explosives from simple TNT to Amatol, C1, C2, C3 and C4 as well as more complex mixtures such as RDX and Semtex. She knew exactly what type she now needed and which components would be required to complete the job.

A half-kilo bag of fertiliser was purchased from a garden centre and a trip to the nearby DIY store provided her with a length of copper pipe and a bag of barbecue charcoal. She also purchased from the same store a clamp-on vice, a battery-powered drill, a box of drill bits, and some strong self-adhesive tape. In addition, she added a hacksaw, a soldering iron, and a reel of soldering wire to her trolley. She left the DIY store satisfied that she had all she needed to create her chosen weapon.

In the kitchen of her apartment, she clamped the vice to the kitchen table and secured the length of copper pipe, then used the hacksaw to cut off a fifty-centimetre length. She then squeezed one end of the pipe closed and soldered the end to seal it. Halfway down the piece of pipe, Farah drilled a small hole into one side of the pipe and inserted the detonator, careful not to press the activation switch on the side. She then soldered the stem of the detonator into the pipe with only a small wire protruding from the end.

Taking a mixing bowl from the kitchen unit, she then poured a batch of charcoal into the bowl and ground it down using a pestle and mortar. Content that she had enough, she picked up the bag of fertiliser and mixed the fertiliser, with its high concentration of potassium nitrate, with the carbon ash. Then she carefully poured the powder mixture into the copper pipe, leaving a small gap at the open end before she then squeezed it closed with the vice and soldered the end to make it airtight. She stood back with a look of satisfaction at what she had manufactured. A series of harmless components used in everyday life, when combined, produced a lethal explosive device known previously as a 'pipe bomb' or, in military talk, an IED – an improvised explosive device.

With the rapid fall in temperature and the shorter days, Farah knew that winter was fast approaching. By late October, this far north saw only seven or eight hours of daylight and a hard frost was routine each morning. She decided to move on her target while his movements were still predictable.

She took a small black backpack and fitted her explosive inside along with the two trigger devices, a roll of adhesive tape, and a pair of night-vision binoculars. Under the cover of darkness, she drove to the entrance of the driveway leading to the lodge and parked in a deserted side street close by. At two thirty in the morning, the streets were empty, and no lights were visible from the few houses in sight. Farah pulled down the woollen hat she wore and transformed it into a full-face mask with only her eyes and mouth visible. She made her way down the long driveway. The storm she had heard forecast on the radio was building fast, accompanied by high winds which would help mask any sounds she made. Farah's senses were on full alert as she made her way towards her target.

Using the night-vision binoculars, Farah observed the small tell-tale glow of a red light coming from a security camera and floodlight system rigged up to be triggered by movement within the arc of the courtyard in front of the house. She crossed over a fence and walked down a grass field using the thick shrubs running parallel with the driveway as cover. She was gambling on the security system being designed to cover the driveway approach and not the surrounding fields. As she neared the house, she crept slowly down the field, covered by the shrub, until she was standing across from Rory McAdam's pick-up truck. She turned to her left, closing the distance between her and the truck and giving a silent prayer that she would not enter the arc of the motion sensors and trigger the lights and alarm or disturb the two dogs.

As she crept towards the truck, she reached out to touch the side of the passenger door, comforted by the feel of the cold steel, knowing that she had made it undetected this far. She checked again with the night-vision binoculars and, satisfied that she could start working undisturbed, she unslung her backpack and removed the two trigger devices. She crawled forward on her belly towards the rear wheel nearest her and carefully removed the protective tape from the power source, setting the pin triggers against the front and back of the rear tyre, ensuring that the pins were fully extended to prevent any early activation. Now, any movement of the pick-up truck forward or backward would compress the trigger pin and complete the electrical circuit, sending the electrical charge to the detonator.

She then crawled under the rear axle and carefully and noiselessly taped the copper pipe to the underside of the vehicle. The last thing she did was the point of highest risk. She reached over to the detonator and, with a delicate hand, felt for the safety switch and slid it down, making the explosive device active, bracing herself with a pounding heart for a premature blast which never came. She lay there for a few minutes, giving a silent prayer and allowing her heart rate to return to normal before strapping on her backpack and quietly retracing her steps back to her car.

As she checked her watch, she saw that the whole operation had taken an hour, but to Farah it had felt like much longer. She drove carefully as snow had begun to fall, and she went through a mental checklist of what she had to do in the apartment before making the long journey back to London.

As dawn began to break the next morning, a layer of snow lay on the frozen ground. She had packed her belongings into her car, emptied the food from the house, and in the darkness of the courtyard, she unscrewed the numberplates of her car and refitted cloned numberplates which had been given to her by an employee of the London-based Mabahith. She slipped out of the car park to head south before sunrise. She left the city of Aberdeen, heading southwards to London, confident that the new car registration plates would confuse any ANPR system used by the British police.

Chapter Twenty-Four

Jaz drew back the curtains and turned to Mac. 'The forecast was right. We have the first snow of winter.'

Mac stood up from watching the news on TV, offering to do the nursery school run. 'I can take the kids in the pick-up. We'll need to use four-wheel drive to get us to the top of the driveway.'

Jaz smiled back. 'No problem, darling, I can do it and be back before you leave for the physio.' With that, Jaz finished getting the kids ready and put on their snowsuits, woollen hats, and gloves while Mac gathered up the packed lunches and stuffed them into the nursery school bags. Mac bent down and kissed young Ella and Cameron.

'Have a great day at nursery and try and stay warm and dry.'

Jaz threw on her winter coat and kissed her husband. 'I won't be long. Get the coffee machine on the go for when I get back.'

Mac smiled as he tossed her the pick-up keys. 'Drive safe, darling. You're very precious to me... and so is your cargo.'

Jaz led the kids out the door, laughing at her husband's words. She clicked the door locks open and loaded the kids into the car seats, fastening them in safely. Then she climbed into the driver's seat, adjusted the seat position and the rear-view mirror before starting up the big V8 engine. She engaged four-wheel drive, let off the handbrake, and edged forward. As the trigger compressed under the tyre, the remote electrical charge ignited the detonator, causing a massive explosion, turning the truck into a fireball, and scattering wreckage all over the courtyard.

The explosion caused the front windows of River Don Lodge to implode, throwing glass all over the inside of the house. Mac had been in the kitchen and was blown across the room by the blast from the explosion. He lay in the corner of the room for a full ten seconds with his brain trying to process what had happened. He had experienced several explosions close to him when serving in the army, but this totally unexpected blast caused a delayed reaction in his senses. As he raised himself to his feet, he saw to his horror that the pick-up truck was engulfed in a fireball.

He rushed outside to be met with a wall of fire fuelled by the petrol from the wrecked vehicle. Mac screamed, 'Jaz, Jaz. Oh my God, Jaz. Ella. Cammy.'

He tried to approach the blazing truck but was beaten back by the fierce fire that consumed what was left of the vehicle. As he stood back, helpless and impotent, he knew inside that nobody could survive such a ferocious explosion followed by a raging inferno.

He slumped against the wall of the house and howled in rage as he realised that this bomb could only have been meant for him and not his family. 'I have brought death and destruction to my family again,' he cried. 'My wife, my kids, gone. Taken from me, so cruel, so callous. I have brought this slaughter upon them.' Mac lay on the ground sobbing uncontrollably until he heard the approaching sirens of the fire engines, police cars, and ambulances making their way to the house, guided by the huge plume of black smoke coming from the burning wreckage of the pick-up truck.

RETRIBUTION

* * *

Farah Halimi had stopped at a motorway service station around late morning to refuel and grab a coffee and a sandwich when she first saw the results of her previous night's work. A TV screen was showing breaking news which headlined a suspected terrorist explosion that had resulted in the deaths of a mother and two young children.

If people had been near enough, they would have heard Farah let out an audible gasp as the shock of the news hit her. Her mind was in turmoil as she thought, *my God, what have I done? This was not what I planned.* She drove the remainder of her journey with her mobile phone switched off, overcome with confusion and agitated at the failure of her plan, and now fearing the wrath of her boss at the Saudi embassy.

Chapter Twenty-Five

Two days after the bomb explosion, now being described by the British media as *mainland Britain's worst terrorist incident in recent years*, very little information had been released by the police regarding the identity of the victims or any surviving members of the ill-fated family. It was almost as if a news blackout had been imposed. On receiving the police report, both Steve Foley, the head of MI6, and Martin Ingram, his Middle East chief, had immediately flown up from London and arranged to meet Rory who had been immediately moved to a safe house. The inconsolable and distraught Rory openly wept to his bosses as he recalled what little information he had of the time leading up to that terrible explosion and subsequent fire. Foley had arranged for Mac's brother and sister-in-law to travel to Aberdeen from their home in Dubai and comfort Rory at this desperate time. An almost impossible task as Rory McAdam plunged into the depths of grief-stricken despair and misery.

Aberdeen estate agent Robert Taylor sat with his wife and watched the horrifying pictures describing the biggest terrorist attack on British soil in recent years. The national news showed pictures of the aftermath of the tragedy and as he watched footage from a drone camera hovering above the site of the bomb blast, it slowly began to dawn on Robert that the site of the scorched patch of earth where the McAdam family car had once stood was a view he had seen before.

He suddenly stood up and turned to his startled wife. 'Oh my God. I think I might know who was behind this.'

His wife gave him a quizzical look. 'What the hell are you talking about, Robert? How could you know or have met any sick person that would do that to a family?'

Robert looked worried but persisted. 'You remember a few months ago I told you about the strange French woman who had plenty of money but insisted on renting a flat in Tillydrone with a view into the River Don and Seaton Park?'

His wife nodded, puzzled as to where this was going. 'The pictures from the drone we just saw on TV were almost identical to the view from the top-floor flat she insisted on renting at any cost.' Robert Taylor paused to gather his thoughts.

'The whole deal, start to finish, was a strange one. She could have rented in the West End, Cults, Bieldside, or Deeside for the budget she had, but she insisted on renting an apartment with a view of Seaton Park. She even paid for the owner to move elsewhere so she could move in right away.'

Robert's heart was racing now as he took a deep breath. 'The view from the top-floor apartment looked right over River Don Lodge... where the bomb went off.'

Colour began to drain from his wife's face. 'I think you should call the police and give them the details so they can check her out.'

As if to convince himself, Taylor went through the whole scenario in his head before convincing himself to call the police. 'It was always something that nagged away inside my head. I remember the owner, Jody Miller, saying to us at the time, "This is too good to be true." I think now she was bloody right.'

Robert Taylor picked up his mobile phone and called the police to give details of Julia Monet, who had rented an apartment overlooking the area where the terrorist bombing had taken place. The policewoman at the other end of the line noted down the details of the property and the woman renting the apartment and passed them to Commander Susan Den of Aberdeen Police, who had taken charge of liaising with British security services on this horrific case. She had a personal involvement with the tragedy, having met Jaz and Rory McAdam on several occasions in the past.

Commander Den was under strict instructions to pass on all information, regardless of how it was graded, to the head of MI5, the head of SO15 Counterterrorism, and Steve Foley, the head of MI6. The police report relating to the call received from an Aberdeen estate agent detailed the address of the empty apartment overlooking River Don Lodge. A detailed search of the Tillydrone apartment had revealed nothing out of the ordinary other than the overwhelming smell of a powerful disinfectant, powerful enough to eliminate fingerprints, skin, sweat, and any traces of DNA. Door-to-door enquiries had revealed that the woman who had occupied the apartment hadn't been seen by anyone for four days – a full two days before the bomb blast.

The onerous task of emptying the community waste bins and searching the week's refuse of the eight families occupying the apartment block turned up a blank writing pad, which would normally have been discarded by the searching forensic officer. The young woman took a closer look at the first page and her sharp eyesight picked up imprints of letters and numbers that had been written on the missing top page.

On nothing more than a hunch, she passed this to the man leading the search team and he carefully bagged the item for further investigation. Under an ultraviolet light, the numbers and letters showed up clearly and a handwriting expert filled in the indentations. The police report included a detailed list of dates and times showing the movements of RM and JM to and from River Don Lodge. The report also included a copy of the passport of the tenant received from Robert Taylor's office, revealing details of the French national Madam Julia Monet, a woman confident that her training in covering her tracks meant she had left no traces of her presence at the apartment.

The SO15 officer handling the case contacted his opposite number in the Paris office of GIGN. He ran the passport details of Julia Monet through their computer systems and, within the hour, confirmed that the passport was a fake. There was no woman of this name born on the date stated on the passport.

The news from Paris triggered a visit by the SO15 commander accompanied by Grampian Police Commander Susan Den to interview Robert Taylor, his assistant Georgia Hewitt, and the owner of the apartment, Jody Miller. All three confirmed that the insistence of Julia Monet to have a view over Seaton Park, which included River Don Lodge, was the overriding factor that had resulted in her paying over the odds for the property as well as an overgenerous payment of rent and utilities to rehouse the owner.

A trawl of CCTV footage of the Tillydrone and Seaton area had resulted in the failure of the police to identify Julia Monet's car. The registration number fed into the DVLA computer gave the owner of the identical white BMW as a David Fraser, a 67-year-old retired doctor of Pentland Road, Watford. A check by police on his supermarket loyalty card confirmed he had been doing his weekly shop on the day of the terrorist attack and had attended a hospital appointment on the previous day. Clearly his registration number had been cloned and used by

Julia Monet. Local police in Watford had visited Fraser and confirmed he had not left the city since last July.

The focus was now on searching footage from traffic cameras for a white BMW hatchback leaving Aberdeen sometime around the time of the bomb explosion, plus or minus three days. An algorithm on the MI5 computer system had been designed to search camera footage for a white BMW hatchback and filter out all other traffic using the roads. The computer produced a list of car registrations, car owners, and their listed addresses, all using the A1 or M6 heading south from Scotland. There was a surprisingly low total during this period and SO15 officers began visiting the nine owners of the vehicles on the list.

Chapter Twenty-Six

Farah Halimi was full of trepidation as she met with her boss at the same park bench they had used before in Hyde Park. She immediately launched into her defence. 'I don't know what went wrong. They always used separate cars before: hers to take the kids to nursery school and his when he visited his physiotherapist and went to the gym. It's been the same every Monday to Friday for the past seven weeks.' She paused, then added, 'Until now!'

Jamal Nasir raised his eyes to the heavens with a pained look on his face. She waited for his reply, fearing a furious reaction to the disaster she had unwittingly created. He held up the palm of his hand to her as he replied in a quiet voice. 'My dear Farah, what is done is done. We cannot change the past, only the present, and the future. Your car has been taken by my assistant, who has arranged for it to be destroyed in a remote area. Give me your passport in the name of Julia Monet and take this new identity.' He reached into his coat pocket and pulled out a new Saudi Arabian passport in the name of Yasmina Al Amin.

'Take this passport and ticket to Riyadh. Wear your hijab when you travel and report to our boss in the Mabahith office.' He handed her an envelope of paperwork before he said, 'Farah, you are still a valuable asset to our kingdom, and you will be reassigned to a new project after your meeting. There is no better place to vanish from the public eye than Saudi Arabia.'

With that, Nasir stood up, leaving Farah with an empty feeling in the pit of her stomach. She could not get rid of the feeling of abandonment from her boss and knew that Saudis, by reputation, had a very low tolerance of failure. Farah was still in possession of her genuine passport and contemplated ignoring her orders and returning to Paris, but quickly dismissed the idea. *Having the British and the Saudis hunting for me would be a recipe for disaster and I would have no safe hiding place anywhere in the world.*

Her journey to Heathrow T4 took over an hour as the taxi slowly made its way through the early morning London rush-hour traffic. She had packed all the jewellery and expensive clothes she'd used in her work in London, but deep inside Farah knew that she would have no use for them in Riyadh. The black full-length shapeless hijab and full-face veil she wore were the only clothes women were permitted to wear in public during her time in the Kingdom of Saudi Arabia.

* * *

The British prime minister David Wallace called a meeting at his country retreat of Chequers. He wanted an update on the progress in tracking down the horrific terrorists which had killed an innocent mother and her two children.

The heads of SO15, MI5, and MI6 joined the prime minister at the conference table, knowing they would have to field some awkward questions and defend their own departments' lack of progress, which was causing a huge amount of negative press in the media, both at home and abroad. The prime minister looked around the table at the three men.

'Gentlemen, last year, before my chancellor's budget, each of you made your case for increased funding.' He saw all three of them drop their eyes to the floor, knowing what was coming next. 'I agreed to all three requests and the chancellor generously increased each of your budgets by fifteen per cent, well above the rate of inflation. You're reasoning for the request for extra funding was *to maintain the level of security to protect the people of the United Kingdom*. So, you can see why I and my government, and indeed the people of our country, are not only disappointed with your lack of progress in finding the killers but outraged at the lack of any breakthrough!' His frustration peaked as his fist slammed onto the table. 'Three weeks have passed since this outrageous and despicable terrorist attack. The British public and I need progress and results, gentlemen!'

The head of SO15, Graham Fraser, felt it was his responsibility to be the spokesman for the three agencies and began with an appraisal of the incident, the investigation into the French woman with the false passport, and the eventual discovery of the burnt-out BMW hatchback that she had used to make her escape.

'Since then, we and the French GIGN have drawn a blank tracking down this woman. We believe she must be getting high-level support, maybe up to diplomatic level.'

David Wallace turned to Fraser. 'Are you saying this was an attack carried out by a foreign government?'

'We can't rule it out,' was Fraser's reply.

Turning to the MI6 chief, he continued, 'According to Steve here, the intended target was undoubtedly MI6 field operator Rory McAdam. Unfortunately, there was a last-minute change of vehicles, resulting in his wife and two children being killed in this appalling attack.'

Steve Foley took up the summary. 'As you will be aware, Rory McAdam was prominent in the team which recently rescued the two Norwegian hostages from the Bekaa Valley in Lebanon. This would have undoubtedly been a blow to the prestige of Hezbollah. McAdam was also a team leader in Operation Babylon, eliminating a senior ISIS leader in Syria. He previously took part in the liquidation of a prominent Saudi prince, who was the main financial backer of ISIS during their brief reign of terror in Iraq and Syria. The latter is more likely to have created a desire for retribution than any other field operations he has participated in.'

There was a stunned silence around the table as the prime minister absorbed this information. He finally replied. 'This Rory McAdam has been a busy boy working on behalf of Her Majesty's Government. It's as well that we in public office don't get involved in the decision-making on the behind-the-scenes security of our country. Ignorance is bliss, as they say.'

David Wallace relaxed a little now, knowing that his three main counterterrorism agencies had done as much as they could under the circumstances, despite the rhetoric in the media about the lack of progress. 'I will ask the Saudi ambassador here in London for assistance, but I already know what the answer will be: evasive and finger pointing at others. Gentlemen, please continue giving this your highest priority and we shall meet again as soon as we have some progress to report on.'

* * *

As the Saudia Airbus climbed into the late morning skies, Farah Halimi tilted her seat back and closed her eyes. She was happy to have escaped London but harboured an uneasy feeling about what lay ahead for her in Riyadh. The six-and-a-half-hour flight felt like a trip to Death Row. She politely declined all offers of food and drinks from the cabin crew. As the aircraft began its final approach into Riyadh, she gave a silent prayer to her god for protection from the powerful men running the Mabahith in this hostile and dangerous country.

As Farah stepped off the plane, she was met by the man who had recruited her in Paris, Khaled bin Ahmed Al Hussein, in his immaculate starched thobe and red-and-white checked abaya.

He greeted her warmly. 'Al salaam alaikum, Farah. Welcome to Riyadh. I will take you to your hotel where you can rest. We will meet tomorrow after morning prayers. I will pick you up at ten o'clock.'

Although Farah was relieved to see her old boss, she was still a very worried woman. 'Alaikum salaam, Khaled. It is nice to see you again,' she replied as she tried hard to mask her concerns. The next twenty-four hours would decide whether she would pay the ultimate price of failure at the hands of the ruthless Mabahith.

* * *

Inside the Mabahith headquarters, Farah sat across the table from the man who held her fate in the balance, her heartbeat racing and her stomach rock hard as he spoke. 'Your failure to execute your mission is a matter of supreme regret to us. We provided you with adequate training and unlimited resources to carry out the retribution as our country and our leaders demanded and yet this man McAdam still walks free – free to carry out more violence on the people of our kingdom.'

He leaned forward and pointed his finger at Farah. 'Free because *you* neglected to follow simple orders to kill this man. Now, because of you, we have the British government asking difficult questions of our ambassador in London.' He stopped to let his words sink in as Farah sat with her head bowed, unable to give him an adequate reply.

'Miss Halimi, I will offer you one last chance to redeem yourself. Khaled Al Hussein has spoken in your defence and is confident that you can succeed if we give you one more chance.'

Farah looked up, startled at this unexpected reprieve. 'I am ready to try again, and I guarantee you success this time. This I promise you.' Confidence started to return as she sat bolt upright. 'I will do whatever is necessary to eliminate Rory McAdam. I will not fail you.'

With that Farah Halimi got a stay of execution and a second chance to eliminate her target. She was left in no doubt that further failure would have catastrophic consequences. She could not help thinking, *you dodged a bullet or more likely a sharp blade.* There was no sense of triumph or even relaxation – the danger was not over, not by a long way.

'You will stay in Riyadh until we are sure you have not been identified before you return to Paris and report to Khaled,' the man told her. He stood up and gathered up some paperwork to signal the end of the meeting. 'Do not fail me again' was his parting warning as she left the room.

* * *

Rory McAdam had plunged into an abyss, his heart and head consumed by the utter devastation that threatened to overwhelm him, caused by the pain and disbelief at his loss. His brother and sister-in-law had immediately flown in from Dubai to console him and slowly, the passage of time dulled the sharp blade of misery and remorse. His immediate boss in MI6, Martin Ingram, accompanied by a trauma psychologist, were regular visitors as they tried to gauge his mental state and disposition. Both knew he faced a stark choice: 'Fight or Flight' was the phrase used in this type of situation.

As Rory McAdam began to come to terms with his loss, there was only one choice for him. He looked skywards as he proclaimed, 'The fight back begins now. I will have retribution for my wife and children.'

The psychologist did not know Rory personally and voiced his concerns about 'Post Traumatic Stress Disorder' and 'Survivor Guilt'. Both were discounted by those who knew Rory McAdam.

Chapter Twenty-Seven

Only in the highest echelons of the American Central Intelligence Agency was the cover name 'Saladin' mentioned. So sensitive was the deep undercover asset that the name had never appeared on any reports or communications, not even to the President of the United States himself. No money or gifts had ever been asked for or offered to Saladin. He had made it clear from day one that what he did was out of conscience, driven by the historical treatment meted out by the brutal regime of the Saudi royal family to one of his family members.

He could never forget or forgive the public execution of his grandfather, who had refused an order to have his oldest daughter spend the night with King Abdullah. The king, during a visit to his grandfather's village, had demanded that the fourteen-year-old should have the privilege to carry a future prince inside her. The girl's father had refused to give over the child and for his refusal and defiance, he had been arrested and taken to Al Turaif, the traditional home of the House of Saud on the outskirts of Riyadh.

The girl's father was held in a darkened prison, starved, tortured, and beaten mercilessly, but still he remained defiant of the royal command. The king's frustration grew into outrage and in a moment of fury, he ordered that the insolent village headman should be used as an example of the king's power. The following day, after Friday prayers, the girl's father was led up to a platform in the main square of Riyadh. With his face swollen and bruised, his nose bloodied and broken, the man, proud of his principles, held his head high as he climbed the wooden stairs.

The crowd watched in a hushed silence as the man was forced down on his knees with his hands bound tightly behind him. The Imam began to recite a prayer from the Koran over the loudspeaker as the executioner picked up his huge, curved sword, gleaming in the midday sun. He pulled back the prisoner's shirt to expose the flesh of his neck and with one almighty sweep of his arms, he thrust down with his sword and removed the head from the body in a fountain of crimson blood. The watching crowd gasped in horror at the sight of the head rolling over the platform. The watching Imam faltered momentarily before he continued with the prayer.

The few people from the prisoner's village who were forced to attend and witness the execution returned to the village with tales of the courage of the man and the horror and injustice of the death sentence. When word of the death of her father reached the fourteen-year-old girl, she walked quietly out of the village and sat in the shade of a nearby palm tree. There she drew out a small knife from her waistband, cut both of her wrists and bled to death, thankful that she would be together with her father again.

The man known to the CIA director as Saladin had taken his mother's family name of Al Zahrani to avoid any problems associated with his grandfather's name. Upon leaving school in Riyadh, he had worked as a policeman before being recruited by the Mabahith. In his early twenties he had been posted to the east coast city of Dhahran, where some excellent undercover work and a little luck saw him uncover a paramilitary cell of Shia dissidents intending to kill prominent Sunni governors and state officials. Even more impressive was Hamed Al Zahrani's discovery that the group had received training and armaments from Saudi's regional rival, the Islamic Republic of Iran. With the cell rounded up and sentenced to death, the Mabahith were able to publicly display evidence of Iranian involvement, much to the delight of the Saudi government.

The work that Al Zahrani had carried out ensured his fast promotion up through the ranks of the Mabahith. Several years later saw him as the Deputy Director of External Operations. Though he enjoyed the high tax-free salary and the many benefits his position gave him, he never forgot the barbaric treatment of his grandfather and the tragic death of his aunt. The blackening of the family name was something he could not forget or forgive, and he sought an opportunity for retribution on the Royal House of Saud.

Chapter Twenty-Eight

'What the hell do you mean *I might have given out his address?*' Giles Rankin could not hide his fury at his nephew. 'For Christ's sake, Andrew, how many screw-ups do you have in you? This bloody mess could cost me my job and my knighthood – and you could end up in prison! What you've done is treasonable!'

Andrew Fox's face turned a deathly shade of pale in front of his uncle, ashamed that he could have been so stupid and naive.

'Who is this woman who manipulated you and had you wrapped around her finger to the extent that you gave out the address of a British security serviceman to a stranger?' As Giles Rankin waited for some kind of response from his distraught nephew, he quickly realised that he would have to find his own way out of this mess and find a solution that moved the spotlight away from him to save his and his family's reputation.

As the operations director at the Ministry of Defence, Giles Rankin was well-connected and highly respected. His role enabled him to come into contact with other high-ranking officials in the defence business, both in the European Union and within NATO. He was particularly friendly with Gio Bartelli, the defence attaché at the Italian embassy in London.

'Gio, I need some help. I need you to pass on some information that will help the British security services trace the people behind a terror attack which took place in Scotland last month.'

The Italian lay down his espresso. 'Giles, this is a strange request. Why can you not pass this information on yourself?'

Rankin gave him a pained look as he squirmed in his chair. 'It's complicated and involves a foolish member of my family unwittingly coming into contact with a woman suspected to be involved in this terrible attack on an innocent family.'

Bartelli was wary about his friend's unusual request. 'What is it you require me to do, my friend?'

Rankin, on seeing a little change in his friend's defensive posture, said, 'Simply pass on an anonymous report to your French counterpart. The woman is a French citizen, just like the one you were screwing a few days ago at my place in Mayfair.'

Gio Bartelli looked astonished as he heard these words from his friend. He sat bolt upright in his chair, confused and agitated. 'How do you know about that?'

Rankin held up his hand and smiled, trying to calm down the hot-headed Italian, and said nothing about the concealed camera he had set up in the bedroom of his apartment.

'You know the old saying, *an investment in knowledge always pays the best interest.* Don't worry, this is just a simple piece of paper with some information to allow the authorities to arrest this criminal and keep my idiotic nephew's name out of it. I can assure you that discretion in all things will serve both of us well in this matter.'

Bartelli could see that he had been backed into a corner and was left with no choice if he was to continue his career at the embassy and enjoy the occasional company of beautiful women introduced to him by Giles Rankin.

* * *

The French GIGN commander made a call to Graham Fraser, his opposite number in SO15. 'I've been passed a handwritten note from an anonymous source which has the name Julia Monet and an address listed as 35A Grosvenor Mews. I'm not sure if this is genuine, but I thought you should have this information in case it could help.'

The SO15 commander thanked him as he scribbled down the address and passed it on to the officer handling the investigations in London. A check in the computer system showed the property owner to be the Qatif Investment Group, with its headquarters listed as Jeddah, Saudi Arabia.

After going through the lengthy process of obtaining a search warrant, based on nothing more than an anonymous tip-off, the police entered the apartment at Grosvenor Mews and found exactly what they had expected. Nothing! The apartment had been cleaned to the standard of a hospital operating theatre.

'It's the same sterile scene encountered in the Aberdeen apartment, sir. No traces of the woman for our forensic teams to work on,' was the gloomy report given by the senior SO15 officer to his commander. Graham Fraser thanked his officer and slumped back into his chair. *I need a lucky break on this one*, he thought.

* * *

The lucky break came in the form of a request for a face-to-face meeting with the SO15 commander from the director of the CIA, who spoke slowly in his Texas drawl, 'I have some information on the recent terrorist attack on the McAdam family in Scotland.'

Fraser's reaction was to sit bolt upright, pen at the ready as the CIA director continued. 'The information I have is highly classified and so sensitive that we have not even involved the president. The source is known only to me and my deputy.'

Fraser's heart rate increased, knowing the Americans would be extremely reluctant to share any information that might compromise such a valuable source. 'I can catch a flight tonight and be in your office tomorrow morning, director,' was Fraser's reply as he tried hard to curb his enthusiasm.

'Very well but come alone as our meeting will be off the record. Look upon it as the latest chapter in our *special relationship.*'

The meeting took place mid-morning the next day at a discreet lounge in Washington's Jefferson Hotel. As Graham Fraser sipped his coffee, awaiting the arrival of the CIA director, he glanced out of the window and saw the unmistakable profile of the White House, two blocks away. Fraser wondered how many other secrets were kept from the President of the United States, who had the title of 'commander-in-chief of the armed forces'. He was thankful that a British prime minister carried no such title nor required constant updates on the security business of the United Kingdom.

The CIA director arrived right on schedule and after the usual formalities about family and mutual friends, he got down to business. 'I'm going to give you a name and address in Paris of the woman who planted the bomb that was meant for your man Rory McAdam. She is currently lying low in Paris using the name Yasmina Al Amin.' The director removed a plain slip of folded paper from his inside pocket and passed it to Fraser. 'This is her address in Paris, and I have given you her real name too.'

Fraser unfolded the paper and read the name Farah Halimi and the address as Rue Edouard, Neuilly-Sur-Seine. 'She's a French-Algerian woman born in Paris, who works for the Saudi embassy in Paris. She is a highly trained field agent, so be extremely careful in your actions.' He looked straight at Fraser before adding, 'It would be a serious error to underestimate this woman.'

Before leaving the table, the director made a request to Graham Fraser. 'Please keep this information as tight as possible and exercise supreme caution in your actions. I don't want to give the Saudis any possible links to the source of this information.'

Fraser shook his hand, thanked the director, and reassured him, 'Only I and Steve Foley will handle this operation. We fully understand the need to protect your source.'

* * *

Less than twenty-four hours since leaving for his meeting in Washington, the SO15 commander and head of MI6 met in a soundproof room deep in the basement of Century House, close to the River Thames at Vauxhall Cross. The headquarters of MI6 could be entered unseen through a tunnel on the far side of the river, guarded by a series of bomb-proof barriers and elite armed police. Fraser passed over the note to Steve Foley. 'She's currently using the name Yasmina Al Amin, although, as we know, her identity can be changed very easily given her employment in the Saudi embassy.'

Fraser paused to let Foley read the note. 'Which brings me round to a long-term and final solution to this attack on Rory McAdam. The way I see it, if we eliminate Halimi, we still have the person at large who ordered the attack.' Foley nodded as he wondered what was coming next. 'Disposing of the woman would be like cutting off the tail of the snake. What I'm proposing is cutting off the head, not just the woman who carried out the attack but the planners of the attack too.'

Steve Foley broke into a smile for the first time in a long time. 'So, we go after Al Hussein, the Mabahith man in Paris?'

Fraser answered immediately. 'Yes, I think we should. I'd like to also take out the London one too, Jamal Nasir. He must have been involved in planning the attack. It would send a hell of a message to the Saudis. Of course, we would have to take out Nasir when he's outside Britain to give us plausible denial.'

Foley's enthusiasm was growing. 'The Saudis will blame Mossad or the Iranians, or both.' Foley thought for a moment before continuing. 'You know, something that's always bothered me about the attack on the McAdam family is how did she know where he lived? We kept his name off the electoral role and there were no records in his name when he purchased the new house. It was done through a shelf company and untraceable back to McAdam. Maybe we can get the answer when we meet Farah Halimi!'

Fraser broke the short silence that followed Foley's rhetorical question. 'Steve, this will be an overseas operation, so your department will have the lead. I'll be available whenever SO15 is needed here. Be careful how you proceed with this as the Americans are obsessed with protecting their asset.'

Foley smiled. 'Rightly so. He must be pretty high up the pecking order to be able to access details on the Halimi woman.'

* * *

Rory McAdam had undergone a full physical and psychological assessment before he attended a meeting with his direct boss, Martin Ingram, accompanied by Steve Foley. Foley opened the proceedings with a pointed question for McAdam. 'The medics have given you a clean bill of health, Mac, but are you sure you're ready to go back into the field? This operation may well mean that one day you might come face to face with the killer of Jasmine and the kids. We may need to keep her alive to help us track down the real people behind the atrocity – the people who instigated it and pointed her in your direction.'

Foley and Ingram studied Mac's body language as they awaited his reply. 'I know there will be questions about my discipline and ability to hold it together if I see this this woman, but I'm professional enough to know my own strengths and weaknesses. It will be a challenge, for sure, but I trust in my training and self-discipline to exercise control and follow my orders.'

Martin Ingram continued. 'The SO15 lads are putting a twenty-four-hour watch on the movements of Jamal Nasir, the Mabahith man at the Saudi embassy in London. We have undercover surveillance set up around the embassy building and around the apartment he uses in Berkeley Square. He won't be able to go for a piss without us knowing about it.'

Foley took up the briefing. 'We've identified the Saudi Mabahith as being behind the attack in Aberdeen. We need to take out Nasir and his Parisian colleague Al Hussein, preferably at the same time.'

Foley let Mac absorb this information for a moment. 'For obvious reasons the hit must be outside the UK, so you can see how we might have to use the woman to arrange for both men to meet up somewhere abroad, and not in Saudi Arabia.'

* * *

The surveillance teams in London tracked Jamal Nasir at his work in the embassy, at his apartment in Berkeley Square, and his sparse social life, which included occasional eating out and two visits to the Emirates Stadium. It appeared that watching Arsenal was Nasir's only life outside of work. In the meantime, the British security services were coming under increased pressure from the media and from politicians in Westminster to bring the terrorists to justice.

MI6 chief Foley addressed the members of the Paris surveillance team. 'You will be posing as tourists in Paris. Stay away from the British embassy as you will not have diplomatic immunity and technically this is an illegal operation carried out on French soil. You will be unarmed, so don't take risks and don't get caught by the French police.' There was a look of surprise among the MI6 surveillance team at the mention of being unarmed before Foley concluded, 'You will be travelling on the Eurostar to get to Paris, avoiding any airport scrutiny. Rory McAdam will be held in reserve here in London in case he is recognised, and the surveillance operation is compromised.'

The stake-out of Farah Halimi's apartment in the Rue Edouard yielded little of value. The woman kept a very low profile and seldom left the apartment. What the surveillance did uncover was that Halimi appeared to have found religion. The team saw her in regular attendance at the Noor-e-Islam Mosque, one of more than seventy mosques in Paris and a brisk twenty-minute walk from her apartment. She attended prayers two or three times a day and four or five times on a Friday.

With round-the-clock surveillance, employing more than thirty field agents in London and Paris, that was seriously eating into the MI6 budget and showing no signs of progress, Steve Foley requested another meeting with the SO15 commander Graham Fraser. 'We're using all our resources to try and find an occasion when both Mabahith men are together outside the country. It's just not happening. Both men and the woman are sitting tight and going about their usual business. This could take a long time and a lot of our valuable resources that we need to reassign to other projects.'

Fraser listened intently. 'What can I do to help you?' he asked.

Foley had been building up to this moment. 'Do you think the asset that the CIA are running in Saudi could arrange for the Paris and London Mabahith men to travel somewhere so we can isolate and terminate both of them?'

Fraser thought about the unusual request before answering. 'That's a very difficult question to answer, Steve. I don't know how the CIA director would take this given the risk of exposure to their asset.'

Foley was growing desperate now and his voice showed it. 'Can we at least ask him if it's possible?'

That evening, Graham Fraser took another transatlantic flight to Washington and met with the CIA director in the same Jefferson Hotel and at the same table as their previous meeting three months ago. The CIA director was taken aback by the request from Fraser. 'I presume there's a sound reason behind this. We have only once asked directly for his assistance and that was several years ago when he pinpointed the location of the Saudi renegade Osama bin Laden. He gave us the location of the bin Laden house in Abbottabad – otherwise we would probably still be searching for him now. In the spirit of co-operation between our countries, I will request his assistance, but I can't promise you a result on this. His security comes first and foremost.'

With that, the meeting moved on to other mundane matters before Fraser caught his overnight flight back to London.

Chapter Twenty-Nine

Saladin visited his regular coffee shop after Friday prayers. The midday temperature in Riyadh was unbearable and only the foolish ventured out in the open. As he returned to the table with his tray of coffee and sweet baklava cake, he noticed that the waiter had included several sachets of salt on his tray. The waiter was the go-between for the CIA to contact Saladin. The Saudi looked over to the counter and caught the eye of the Filipino who had served him. A discreet nod towards the men's washroom signalled that he needed to pass on a message.

Saladin sipped half of his coffee before making his way to the men's room where he was handed a folded message. No words were exchanged or were necessary. Both men knew the high-risk business they were engaged in. Discovery would bring a torturous and agonising death.

Back in the safety of his luxury villa on the outskirts of Riyadh, Saladin read the message twice more to make sure he'd understood what his American friends were asking him to do. He had ridden his luck when he had given them the location of Osama bin Laden, but he was no fool. He knew that each time he passed on information, the closer to discovery he would be. Things had been very quiet for the Mabahith in Europe since the failed attempt on the life of British agent Rory McAdam.

He also knew that the Saudi regime would not rest until they had their revenge, unless they received a message that only the Saudi royals would understand. He would be the unseen courier to deliver this message.

* * *

To break both Jamal Nasir and Khaled Al Hussein out of their normal routine, Foley decided to have one of his surveillance team break into Farah Halimi's apartment in Paris, leaving no obvious signs of the intrusion but a photograph of Jasmine McAdam and her two children. 'This should raise the alarm and might provoke the Saudis into some rash decision-making.' Steve Foley thought only something as drastic as this would panic the Mabahith away from the safety of their embassies.

'We think we can get both Al Hussein and Nasir on the move, which will give us a chance to take them out. I can't go into details on the where and when, but once we know a date and a location, we will have to move very quickly. It will be a matter of hours' notice, not days, so we need to cover every option to take them down.'

* * *

The Maghrib, or sunset prayer, finished at around eight thirty in Paris. Farah made her way to the door of the women's prayer room, put her shoes back on, tied her headscarf over her head, and began the walk back to her apartment, at peace with herself and enjoying the warm Parisian evening.

She entered the apartment block and climbed the stairs to her second-floor apartment. Before entering, she checked the tiny tell-tale thread she had fixed between her door and the doorpost. As usual she gave a slight sigh of relief, raised her eyes to the heavens, and silently thank Allah. The thread was still there undisturbed, ensuring that nobody had entered the apartment in her absence.

Farah unlocked the door, removing her headscarf and her coat before entering her lounge. Something didn't feel right as she entered the room. Her eyes were drawn towards an object which caused her to take a step backwards, her eyes blinking rapidly and an ice-cold river of blood flowing through her body. She felt dizzy and her legs went weak as she stared at a photograph of a woman and two children. It took a few moments to comprehend just what she was looking at before she gasped in horror.

She quickly went over to a drawer and removed her pistol before checking the kitchen and bathroom to ensure the intruder had gone. She turned around, bolted the door behind her, and immediately called Khaled Al Hussein in Paris on his mobile phone.

Al Hussein grimaced as he looked at the number and saw who the incoming caller was. 'Farah, it's Friday, my only day off.'

Farah cut in, ignoring her manners. 'The apartment has been broken into and they left a photograph of the McAdam family! I am not safe here any longer. They know where I live!'

There was a stunned silence on the other end of the line before Al Hussein finally spoke. 'How could this be? You are in one of our safe houses.'

'Well, it's not safe anymore. I need out tonight, but I am afraid to go out again.'

'You must be under surveillance. Wait there and I will arrange for a team to collect you and move you to the embassy.'

Later, after contemplating this news, Al Hussein picked up

his mobile phone and gave his colleague Jamal Nasir in London the grave news.

'What can we do? This is very unexpected, and the woman is panicking.'

Nasir listened with growing dread, bewildered that the safe house had been compromised and an intruder, undoubtedly from MI6, had entered the apartment and left a photograph of her victims.

'We must talk to the director. He needs to advise us of the next step. This is a very serious development.'

The video call linked between Riyadh, London, and Paris lasted around fifteen minutes and many wild scenarios were thrown around by Al Hussein and Nasir. Finally, the director put a halt to the theories being discussed. 'Gentlemen, we have tried once to kill this man, and we failed. We need to revise our plans and develop a solution that will finally bring justice to our ruling family. Come to Riyadh and we will discuss it in the comfort and security of our headquarters.'

There was agreement from both men before the director added, 'I will arrange for an aircraft to pick you up in five days' time, first to London, and then Paris, before heading to Riyadh.'

* * *

The information passed on by Saladin included the date, locations, and estimated times the aircraft would collect the two Saudi Mabahith chiefs, as well as the aircraft type and registration number. The coded message was passed directly to the CIA director in Washington, who in turn passed the information to his counterpart at MI6.

Steve Foley and Martin Ingram together decided that Rory McAdam needed some sort of closure on the appalling tragedy that his family had suffered. They made a secure phone call to Rory McAdam and gave him the instructions to travel to Paris and contact the surveillance team, along with the contact details of two French assets who worked at Le Bourget airport outside Paris.

The two men had occasionally passed on names or flight details of passengers when requested by British intelligence but had never been tasked with direct action. The requests were accompanied by cash payments discreetly passed on to the men by a member of staff at the British embassy in Paris.

Rory knew they had only three days to organise a plan to eliminate the two Saudi nationals. Mac arranged to meet the two airport workers in Bar Elysée, a working men's bar in the Montmartre district of northern Paris. After a brief introduction, he got down to business, acutely aware of the tight window of opportunity he had been given. He passed them a slip of paper which described the type of aircraft, the registration number, and the estimated departure time from Le Bourget airport.

'When this executive jet arrives from Oxford airport on Wednesday, it will have one passenger already aboard. The plane will pick up one more, a Saudi national with known links to terrorism. I need to get access to the luggage hold.' Both men looked at each other and nodded simultaneously.

The smaller of the two men smiled back at Rory. 'Monsieur, for the right price, I can guarantee you will get access to the aircraft.' He turned and patted his colleague on the back. 'Hugo here will have a day off and you will be loading cargo for this aircraft. You will be carrying out this task alone while I engage the pilot in conversation. I have worked many times before on this type of plane and I am familiar with the layout.'

Bruno Roche leaned forward and lowered his voice. 'The price will be more than our usual fee, but I know you will have already considered this. I will collect you outside this bar at seven o'clock on Wednesday morning. I will bring Hugo's security pass, baseball cap, and hi-vis jacket. You will have no trouble with the security guards as I will engage them in conversation while you swipe your pass and enter through the staff access door.'

Mac replied, 'You will have played a part in ridding the world of two of the top terror organisers known to the Western world,' he said. Both Frenchmen were known to hold extreme right-wing views and looked pleased to play their part.

Hugo and Bruno drained their glasses of wine and gave Rory a cheery wave as they both left the bar. Rory sat there thinking of this highly risky plan. *I have not worked with these guys before, but Foley assures me they are very good.*

Chapter Thirty

As the pilot taxied to a halt after the short flight from Oxford airport, he cut the engines and left his seat to open the main door, which unfolded a set of steps from the aircraft down to the ground. The jet borrowed from the Saudi royal fleet was painted white apart from its black serial number. The young co-pilot remained in his seat, strapped in and polishing the lens of his Ray-Ban's to the point of wearing down the glass. Mac watched discreetly from the baggage shed as the second passenger accompanied by a woman approached the aircraft and climbed aboard to be welcomed by the pilot and the other passenger.

Farah Halimi had been a last-minute addition to the passenger list at the suggestion of the Mabahith director back in Riyadh. As Mac pushed a luggage trolley towards the rear of the aircraft, Farah was looking out from her window seat and saw the baggage handler approaching the aircraft. Mac kept his head down with the peak of the baseball cap shielding the upper part of his face.

Farah's heartbeat started racing as she looked at the man approaching and shifted in her seat to try and get a better view of the baggage handler. Something at the back of her mind had triggered an uneasy feeling as she tried to focus on the part of the face that was visible. Something was familiar about him as her eyes darted up and down the length of his body, then he disappeared from view and started loading the passengers' suitcases. Farah told herself to stop overreacting to the slightest thing. She would be accused of being paranoid and seeing ghosts by her bosses if she said anything. Still, she could not get rid of that nagging feeling about the baggage handler.

After securing the luggage in the hold, Mac reached into his inside pocket, withdrew the device, and clipped it onto the air tube leading from the aircraft's compressor to the main cabin, then closed the cargo door. Bruno got the manifest signed by the pilot before disembarking and giving the pilot the thumbs up to signal that the ground crew had completed all formalities.

The pilot got permission to start his engines and took off a few minutes later on a south-easterly heading, to fly over the islands of Sardinia and Sicily, climbing at an altitude of 45,000 feet. As he passed through the 20,000 feet mark, the pilot was unaware of a small popping noise that came from the device that severed the air tube which carried air from a compressor to the cockpit and passenger compartment and began a decrease in cabin pressure as the plane's altitude increased.

The failure to increase cabin pressure within the aircraft and the resultant reduced levels of oxygen in the bloodstream induced fatigue, drowsiness, and would lead to hypoxia.

Jamal Nasir was the first person to lose consciousness, but as Farah glanced over to the man sitting across from her, she presumed he was sleeping, tired from his early morning start in London. She then glanced behind her and saw that Khaled Al Hussein was also fast asleep, and she relaxed knowing that the two men who held her life in their hands were dormant for now.

Farah herself felt very tired but put this down to the sleepless nights since she had discovered the McAdam family photograph in her apartment. An hour into her flight, Farah got up from her seat to use the toilet. As she approached the toilet, she glanced into the cockpit and noticed the pilot and co-pilot both slumped in their seats and appearing to be dozing. A sudden panic came over her as her chest tightened and she started struggling to breathe. *No, no, no, this isn't happening!* She knew immediately that this was very wrong, and her mind flashed back to the baggage handler in Paris.

Farah moved towards the pilot and tried to shake him awake and was similarly unsuccessful with the co-pilot. The growing feeling of terror inside her made her shout at the pilots. The lack of any response caused her to scream as tears began flow. Farah started to hyperventilate and finally succumbed to the lack of oxygen and fell unconscious.

According to the flight plan submitted to the French air traffic control, the pilot should have changed course after passing over the island of Crete, which would have taken him on a direct heading over Egyptian airspace, before a final adjustment for Riyadh airport.

Flying on autopilot after levelling out, the now unconscious pilot failed to alter course into Egyptian airspace, and the aircraft continued towards Israeli airspace. Concern grew among Israeli air traffic control as the plane began to show up on their radar screens. The intruder was identified as a Saudi Arabian-registered private aircraft and repeated attempts by the Israelis to communicate with the pilot were met with silence other than the constant hum of static.

The officer in charge of the coastal radar station at Ashdod was informed that the Saudi aircraft was on a direct heading towards Israel's highly sensitive nuclear plants at Beersheba and

Dimona, deep in the Negev Desert. Panic began to grow rapidly within the people running the air traffic control radar station.

The radar officer telephoned the duty officer at the Rishon Le Zion military air force base and quickly explained the situation about a Saudi Arabian aircraft which had entered Israeli airspace and the pilot refusing to respond to calls to alter his course. The commander of the airbase immediately contacted the general of the Israeli Defence Force in Tel Aviv and briefed him on the situation. The general issued a *Code Red* alert and gave the instruction, 'Scramble the fighters and shoot the plane down if it continues to approach the Negev,' was the brisk orders the colonel received.

Four F16 jet fighters were scrambled and roared down the runway, taking off in pairs, and set a course to head off the Saudi jet, which was failing to respond or alter its course. The senior officer led the group of four fighters on an intercept course which would see them come into visual contact with the Saudi aircraft in seven minutes. All of Israel's pilots were highly trained and highly motivated individuals and this group of four were no exception. As they came within view of the intruder, the leader instructed his three pilots to circle above the Saudi aircraft as he closed in to try and make visual contact with the pilot. Three times the senior officer tried to attract the attention of the pilot and the co-pilot and three times he was ignored.

The jet was fast approaching the coastline of Israel and would soon be entering Israel's restricted airspace around the nuclear facilities. The lead pilot turned his aircraft for a final time, bringing his fighter above and behind the stricken Saudi jet before he fired a single hellfire air-to-air missile.

The missile hit the Saudi jet between the tailplane and the starboard engine, causing the aircraft to explode in mid-air and plunge to the earth, trailing fire and debris before crashing into the desert.

It was pointless to look for survivors, but Israeli emergency crews were able to quickly reach the scene and put out the fire in the remains of the smashed fuselage. Israeli crash investigators, after a thorough search of the wreckage, were later able to confirm that four Saudi nationals and a French woman were aboard the aircraft when it was shot down. No cause was ever established as to the purpose of the intrusion into Israeli airspace, but a press release for the IDF confirmed they had intercepted a suspected suicide attempt to crash the plane into a nuclear facility in the Negev Desert.

The statement confirmed: *Our heroic defence personnel were able to identify, intercept, and destroy a terrorist attempting an airborne suicide attack on an establishment which is crucial to the protection of the state of Israel. There were similarities between this attempt and the 9/11 attack on our American brothers where fifteen of the nineteen terrorists were Saudi Arabian nationals.*

Chapter Thirty-One

The meeting in Century House took place three days after the statement released by the Israeli Defence Force. MI6 chief Steve Foley could not hide his satisfaction at the outcome and fallout of the incident. Addressing the Middle East chief Martin Ingram and Rory McAdam, he raised his cup of coffee in a toast.

'Gents, this is a perfect ending to a horror episode for everyone here.'

He paused and turned to McAdam. 'Especially you, Rory.'

A grim-faced Rory nodded in agreement as Foley increased the tone of his voice.

'The Israelis have been praised by the Americans for an exceptional response to a potential catastrophic terror incident'. He paused before adding,

'A suicide attack on a nuclear facility is the ultimate terror weapon, and the Israeli's responded with their customary maximum force'.

'The Saudis are extremely angry at losing two top Mabahith directors, plus two pilots, and an unnamed female passenger. They are adamant on laying the blame firmly on the door of the Israelis.' He took a sip of water before continuing,

'There has been no explanation from the Saudi government as to why the plane was so far off its planned route. It will remain an unsolved mystery. The wreckage has now been removed and will never be seen again.'

'The British government and security agencies are under no suspicion, and we have distanced ourselves from any knowledge or involvement in the incident.'

Foley concluded, 'We could have eliminated the Saudis anywhere, but the success wasn't just in the execution, but in the evasion afterwards.'

Chapter Thirty-Two

After the incident of the downed Saudi jet over Israeli airspace, the director of the CIA received a surprise message from Saladin in the form of a coded text. It simply gave the name of Andrew Fox and asked for the name to be passed on to British intelligence.

The name was passed on from Foley to his domestic counterpart at MI5, who initiated a thorough investigation into the man employed at the Ministry of Defence. Checks were made on his phone records, credit cards, emails, and bank accounts in the last three years since he'd resigned his commission from the army.

Under caution, he was asked to explain regular and significant payments from a Middle East bank, phone calls, messages, gifts, and a trip to Paris with a French-Algerian woman – Juliet Monet. Andrew Fox floundered, unable to give a plausible or believable explanation for the regular cash payment from the Saudi National Bank. He admitted to having been in a brief relationship with a French woman, Juliet Monet, before she disappeared from his life, and was astounded to be told she worked for the Saudi security services. He broke down when told that the information he had passed to her had led to the horrific deaths of Rory McAdam's wife and two young children.

* * *

Giles Rankin was hauled into a meeting with the head of the MOD, along with Steve Foley and the head of MI5. Rankin sat opposite all three men as he listened in horror to the evidence against his nephew, who Rankin recommended to be hired by the Ministry of Defence. An angry Steve Foley addressed Rankin.

'You can forget about your bloody knighthood.'

'You and your idiotic fool of a nephew are extremely fortunate not to be on trial for treason and to be facing a long stretch in prison.'

'Only the need for us to keep this whole episode classified is saving you.'

'You will resign with immediate effect and retire to your stately home.'

With that, Foley slammed his folder closed, stood up, and left the room still incensed that their reckless and foolish actions had led to the deaths of three innocent lives.

Two weeks after Giles Rankin had resigned his position as operations director at the Ministry of Defence, Rory McAdam approached his boss and requested a leave of absence. 'Mac, you take as much time off as you need. You have been under huge stress and a break will do you good. Let me know when you are ready to return.' They shook hands and Rory McAdam strode out of Century House with his shoulders pushed back and a determined look and unmistakable sense of purpose in his demeanour.

Chapter Thirty-Three

Andrew Fox felt bitter and angry towards the French woman he knew as Juliet Monet. His naivety had let her use him to obtain the information she needed and then drop him like a stone. The investigation by MI5, followed by the dismissal from his job in the Ministry of Defence, left Fox with no prospects of ever gaining employment in Britain again. This was further compounded by his uncle Giles having to resign his job at the MOD. The tongue lashing he received from his mother had left him in no doubt that he had let the family down and cost his uncle his knighthood.

Fox had sold his apartment in London and the proceeds of the sale were likely to be his sole income for the foreseeable future. He had moved to a small remote cottage in Devon which belonged to his mother and was occasionally used as a holiday home by members of the family.

After a cold and bleak winter spent in the cottage, Andrew Fox now began to feel a little more positive within himself as spring brought sunshine and warmth. The depression he had initially felt had now given way to hope. He had put his energy into clearing a piece of land at the back of the cottage and the physical effort of cutting down trees and clearing the ground had a cleansing effect on his mood.

After a hard day's work with the axe and chainsaw, the

clearing was now complete, and he rewarded himself after supper with his fourth large glass of Merlot and a hot bath overflowing with soap bubbles. Fox lay relaxing in his bath with a warmth spreading through his body, sipping his wine and listening to classical music.

He was completely oblivious to the sound of Mac applying a rubber suction pad and using a diamond-tipped glass cutter to slice through and remove a glass panel on the front door. Rory McAdam slipped his hand inside and unlocked the door.

Earlier, Mac had laid on a nearby hilltop hidden from sight, observing Fox's comings and goings. He had peered through his binoculars as Fox returned to the cottage and prepared and ate his supper. Mac then saw him go to the bathroom where he began to notice a trail of steam coming from the bathroom ventilator.

Mac had left his cover and crept up to the cottage where he heard a steady stream of water running in the bathroom accompanied by the sound of classical music. He knew that Fox was alone in the cottage and quietly entered the house. He made his way towards the source of the music and paused outside the bathroom door, feeling a strange serenity knowing that he would now bring some closure for Jasmine and his children.

Mac was no expert on classical music but recognised the tune 'O Fortuna' beginning to play. He opened the door and saw Andrew Fox lying in the bath with his back to Mac. With the music building to a crescendo, Mac closed the gap between him and his target. He lay his gloved left hand on Fox's head and pushed the head under the water. The shock to Andrew Fox caused him to instinctively raise his arms up out of the water to try and react to the force pressing his head under. Mac grabbed his wrists with his right hand and pushed down harder, causing

Fox to swallow huge gulps of bathwater. The terror he felt forced his eyes to bulge out of their sockets and his heart to race. Fox tried to scream and only succeeded in swallowing more water.

Fox kicked out with his legs in vain as his lungs began to fill up with bathwater, but Mac held his head under with an iron grip. Before a minute had passed, Andrew Fox slowly slid deeper under the water as all life had seeped from his body. Rory McAdam felt a rush of adrenalin course through him knowing that retribution had been attained and left the cottage the same way he had entered.

EPILOGUE

Devon police, investigating the death of Andrew Fox, sent a report to the coroner in Plymouth, who concluded that the cause of death was accidental drowning compounded by excessive consumption of alcohol. Before the police cordon around the cottage had been lifted, a call was placed to a specialist glazing company from Southampton who were approved to carry out work for the Royal Navy. A glazier attended to the cottage front door, removed the remains of the damaged glass panel, and replaced it with an identical panel.

After his four-month leave of absence, Rory McAdam returned to active duty with MI6 and immediately started work on infiltrating the Houthi movement in Southern Yemen. The Houthis were starting to menace shipping entering and exiting the Suez Canal and adding significant costs in time and money for commercial shipping in the region.

Acknowledgements

Writing a follow-up to *Eye for an Eye* has been a tough task and I have been helped along the way by friends and family. I would like to thank my publisher, Duncan Lockerbie of Lumphanan Press, for his assistance and words of encouragement. I also received invaluable help from my editors Elaine Smith and Gale Winskill.

My friends John McDonald and Garth Perry gave me excellent feedback and suggestions, some of which I took on board and some I declined (sorry John). A special thanks to my wife Joan and our three daughters Lyne, Jill, and Emma who were tireless in their support and encouragement in writing this story, especially as it got near to completion.